ASTRONOMY TODAY

The RANDOM HOUSE
LIBRARY OF KNOWLEDGE™

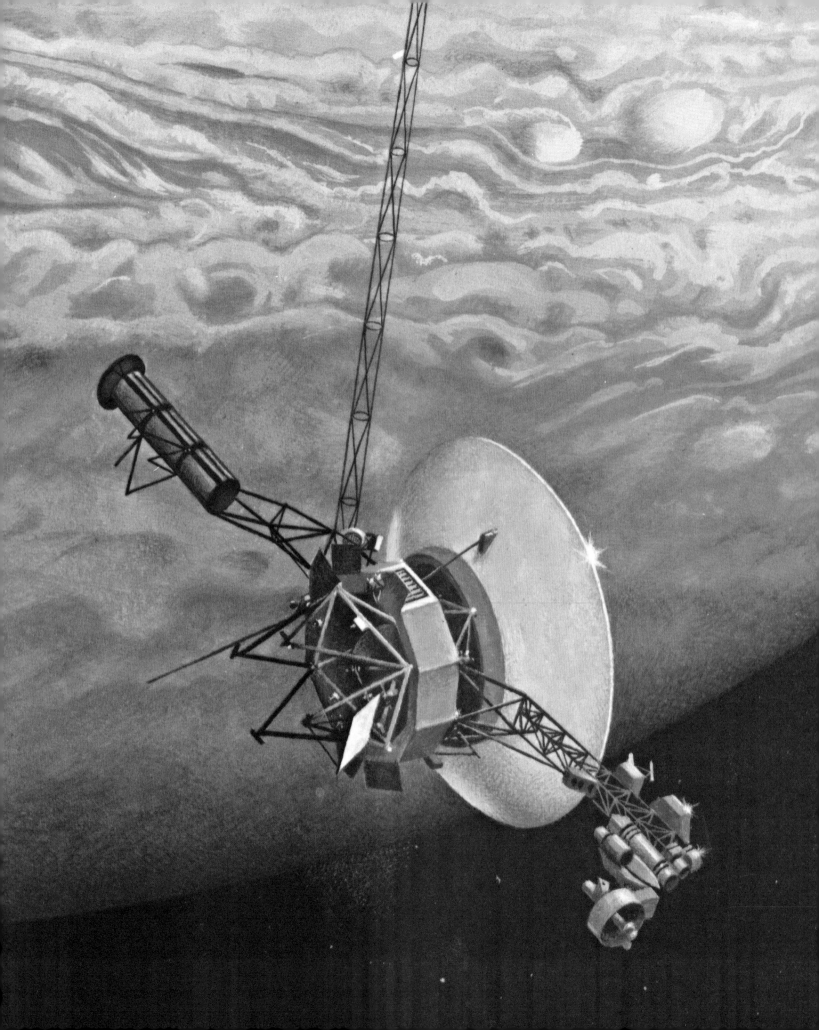

ASTRONOMY TODAY

BY Dinah L. Moché, PH.D.

Professor of Physics and Astronomy,
Queensborough Community College of the
City University of New York

ILLUSTRATED BY Harry McNaught

 RANDOM HOUSE

NEW YORK

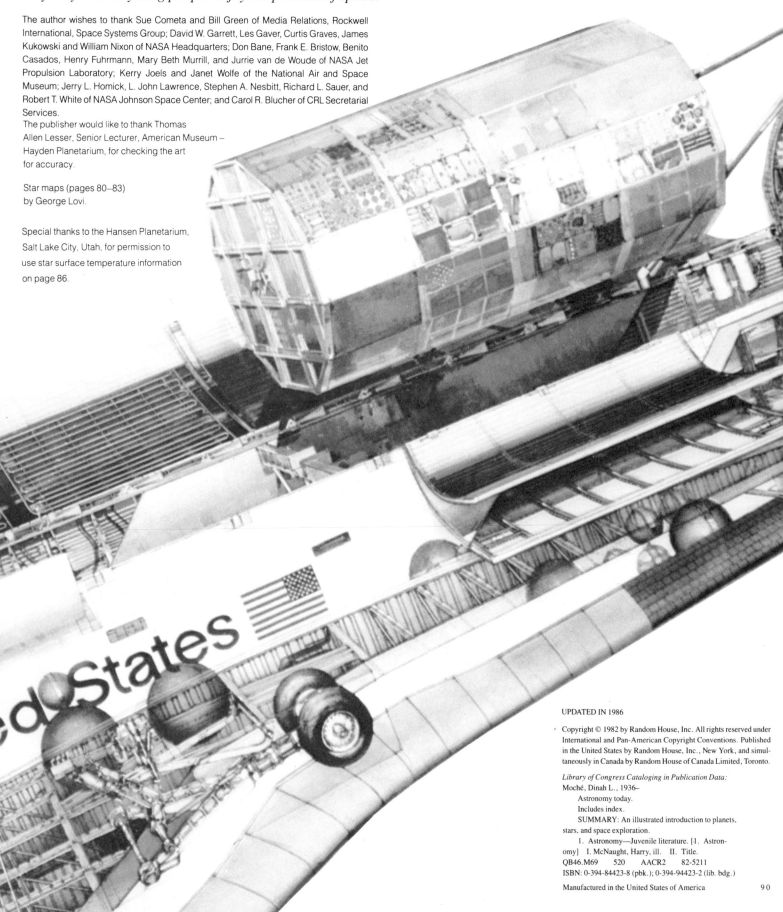

To my daughters, Rebecca and Elizabeth—
may they and all young people enjoy the promise of space.

The author wishes to thank Sue Cometa and Bill Green of Media Relations, Rockwell International, Space Systems Group; David W. Garrett, Les Gaver, Curtis Graves, James Kukowski and William Nixon of NASA Headquarters; Don Bane, Frank E. Bristow, Benito Casados, Henry Fuhrmann, Mary Beth Murrill, and Jurrie van de Woude of NASA Jet Propulsion Laboratory; Kerry Joels and Janet Wolfe of the National Air and Space Museum; Jerry L. Homick, L. John Lawrence, Stephen A. Nesbitt, Richard L. Sauer, and Robert T. White of NASA Johnson Space Center; and Carol R. Blucher of CRL Secretarial Services.

The publisher would like to thank Thomas Allen Lesser, Senior Lecturer, American Museum – Hayden Planetarium, for checking the art for accuracy.

Star maps (pages 80–83) by George Lovi.

Special thanks to the Hansen Planetarium, Salt Lake City, Utah, for permission to use star surface temperature information on page 86.

Library of Congress Cataloging in Publication Data:
Moché, Dinah L., 1936–
    Astronomy today.
    Includes index.
    SUMMARY: An illustrated introduction to planets, stars, and space exploration.
    1. Astronomy—Juvenile literature. [1. Astronomy] I. McNaught, Harry, ill. II. Title.
QB46.M69   520   AACR2   82-5211
ISBN: 0-394-84423-8 (pbk.); 0-394-94423-2 (lib. bdg.)

Manufactured in the United States of America

Illustration on this page and pages 76, 77, NASA.

CONTENTS

Introduction	6
Night and Day	8
The Changing Sky	10
The Seasons	12
Starlight	14
Optical Telescopes	16
Launch Vehicles	18
Satellites and Probes	20
The Solar System	22
The Planets	24
The Sun	26
Our Closest Star	28
Mercury	30
Venus	32
Planet Earth	34
Drifting Continents	36
Aerospace	38
The Moon	39
Phases, Tides, and Eclipses	40
Robot Explorers	42
Apollo Mission Profile	44
Mars	46
Exploring Mars	48
Jupiter	50
Jupiter's Moons	52
Saturn	54
Saturn's Moons	56
Uranus	58
Neptune	60
Pluto	61
Asteroids	62
Comets	64
Meteors	66
Humans in Space	68
Space Stations	70
Space Shuttle	72
Space Shuttle Mission Profile	74
Space Shuttle Orbiter	76
Stargazing	78
–Spring Star Map	80
–Summer Star Map	81
–Autumn Star Map	82
–Winter Star Map	83
Stars	84
H-R Diagrams, Binaries, and Variables	86
Evolution of Stars	88
The Milky Way Galaxy	90
Neighboring Galaxies	92
The Universe	94
Index	95

Introduction

THE STARS YOU SEE on a clear, dark night are trillions of miles away and their light travels many years before it reaches your eyes. Earth is just a speck in the vast universe.

Earth is part of the solar system, a family of planets with their moons plus countless objects all circling the Sun. Astronomy today is bursting with exciting discoveries, from life in space shuttles and space stations to spectacular closeups of giant Jupiter and dazzling Saturn.

Our solar system belongs to a great system of over 100 billion widely separated stars called the Milky Way Galaxy. The Sun, Earth with its human passengers, and all the other stars in the Galaxy race around its center. The Milky Way Galaxy is so huge that you would have to travel at least 100,000 years to go across it at lightspeed.

Sophisticated telescopes and instruments provide fascinating pictures of the Milky Way Galaxy, with its many strange objects and violent events powered by energy sources not yet used on Earth. Today's astronomers search for possible black holes, research puzzling objects such as quasars, and listen for messages from intelligent beings who may be on planets circling distant suns.

Beyond our Milky Way Galaxy are billions of other galaxies, each containing billions of stars. These galaxies are extremely far apart from each other. The intergalactic space between them is practically empty. A trip to the closest galaxy like our own would take some two million years at lightspeed.

This book will help you enjoy stargazing. It has the newest information about space, together with the most important ideas from yesterday and thrilling plans for tomorrow. The star maps on pages 80–83 and the fact columns throughout the book will guide you as you explore the wonders of space yourself.

Our solar system is just a speck (pinpointed by a red dot) in the Milky Way Galaxy. There are billions of other galaxies in our universe.

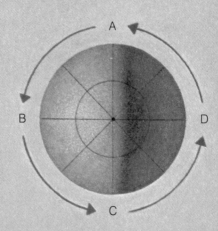

Imagine that you are far out in space, looking down on Earth's North Pole (above). There are four spots marked on Earth—A,B,C, and D. Local time at point A is sunrise, while it is the middle of the day at point B, sunset at C, and midnight at D.

In the illustration at the left, the side of Earth facing the Sun has daylight while the other half has the darkness of night. As Earth rotates from west to east the places in sunlight gradually turn away from the Sun and into the night side.

Night and Day

THE SUN IS A STAR and shines all the time. It lights the side of Earth that faces it. Because Earth rotates, or spins, once every 24 hours, your part of the world has day and night regularly. If Earth were still, half of the world would always be in sunlight and the other half would always be in darkness.

If you observed a clear sky for 24 hours, you would see the Sun rise in the east early in the morning and set in the west in the evening. During the night you would see stars move by.

The Sun and stars don't really move across the sky.

They just appear to because you observe them from the spinning Earth.

When your part of the world turns toward the Sun, you have sunrise in the east. As Earth rotates during the day the Sun seems to go across the sky. Glare from sunlight scattered by the atmosphere hides the stars.

When your part of the world turns away from the Sun, you have sunset in the west. At night Earth blocks the sunlight. Then you see stars shining in space. As Earth turns during the night the stars seem to go across the sky.

Night and day are large divisions of time. Long ago people used the position of the Sun to gauge smaller divisions. The time when the Sun was at its highest in the sky was called noon. The period of time from noon of one day to noon of the next day was divided into 24 hours. This method worked well until people began to travel long distances by train.

As early trains traveled east or west, stations along the way had different local times. The time at which noon occurred was different at each location because Earth rotates from west to east. Places in the eastern United States turn toward the Sun before places in the west do. It is local noon at a spot in the east before it is local noon at a place 1,000 miles (1,600 kilometers) to the west. A standard for telling time everywhere in the world was badly needed to avoid confusion.

In the late 1800s an international system for telling time was agreed upon. The world was divided into 24 equal time zones, each one hour apart. Each time zone has a standard time. All places in a time zone use the same standard time instead of their local time.

Standard time is measured from the meridian of longitude that passes through the Greenwich Observatory just outside of London, England. (Meridians are the lines on a globe running from pole to pole.) As you go west, it is one hour earlier in each time zone. It is one hour later in each time zone to the east.

The United States and possessions are divided into eight standard time zones. Many places use daylight-saving time part of the year. Clocks are set one hour ahead of the standard time there. Then there is more sunlight when people are awake.

The three drawings on the right represent views of Earth at three different times. Drawing A shows a view one hour earlier than B, and B shows a view one hour earlier than C. In A, City 1 is experiencing sunrise. Cities 2, 3, and 4 are still in darkness. In B— one hour later—the globe has turned 15° of longitude toward the sunlight. City 1 has had sunlight for one hour, and City 2 is just now experiencing sunrise. In C, City 1 has had sunlight for 2 hours, City 2 has had sunlight for 1 hour, and City 3 is just now experiencing sunrise. City 4 will not experience sunrise for another hour.

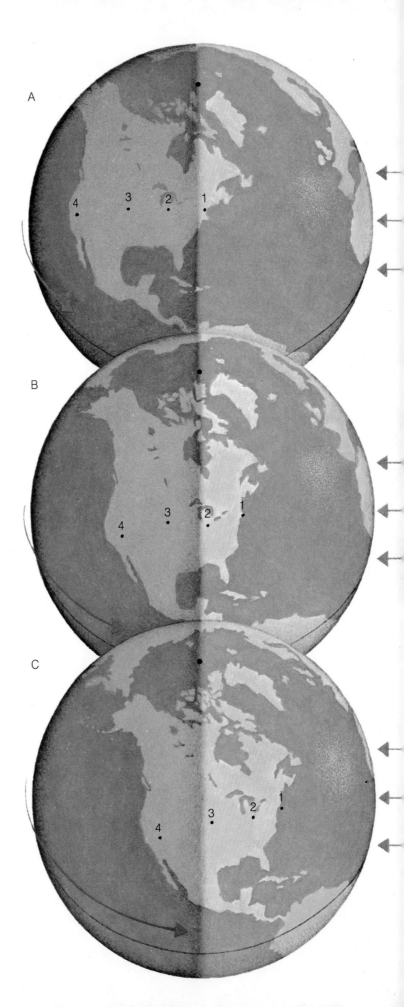

The Changing Sky

ON A VERY CLEAR, dark night you can see about 2,000 stars. If you go stargazing, you'll see that the stars seem to move across the sky during the night. They seem to move because Earth is turning.

If you were to observe the sky regularly for a whole year, you would see some different stars each season. Your view of space keeps changing because Earth revolves, or travels around the Sun. Every hour Earth speeds more than 67,000 miles (107,000 kilometers) along its orbit, or path.

Imagine drivers in the Indianapolis 500 Memorial Day race. As the drivers speed around the track, they see different parts of the scenery at the edge of the track. In the same way, you see different stars as Earth speeds along its orbit around the Sun.

Earth takes twelve months to orbit once. After one year Earth is back where it started. Then you see the same stars again.

For stargazing, you need a different star map in summer, fall, winter, and spring. On pages 80–83 of this book you will find special star maps to guide you in each of the four seasons.

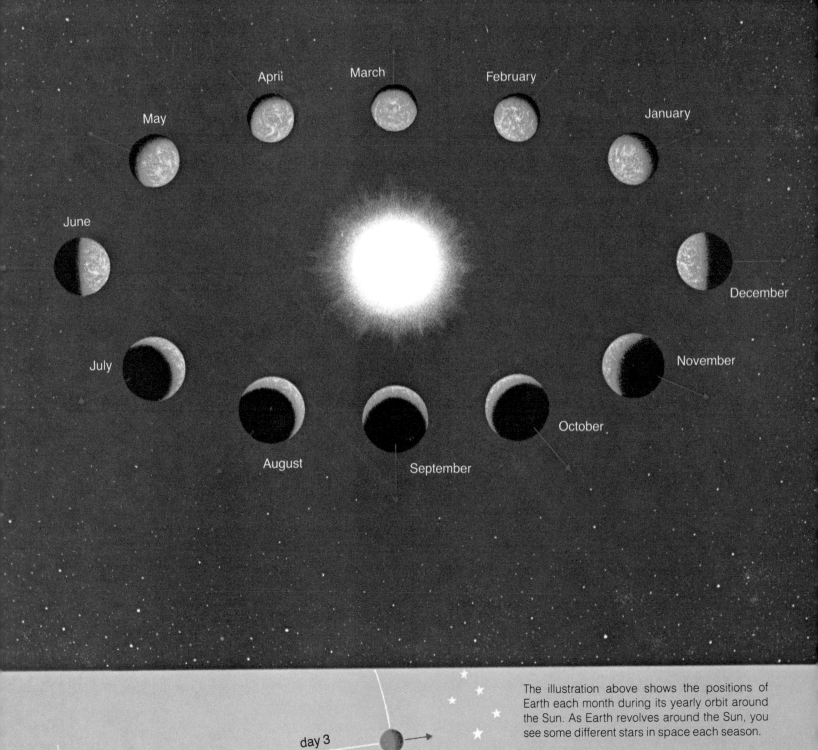

May

April

March

February

January

June

December

July

November

August

September

October

day 3

day 2

day 1

The illustration above shows the positions of Earth each month during its yearly orbit around the Sun. As Earth revolves around the Sun, you see some different stars in space each season.

The illustration on the left shows Earth's location in its orbit on three consecutive days. Because the spinning Earth travels around the Sun, you get a slightly different view of space each night. You would see a star rise four minutes earlier on day 2 than it did on day 1. On day 3 you would see the star rise eight minutes earlier than it did on day 1.

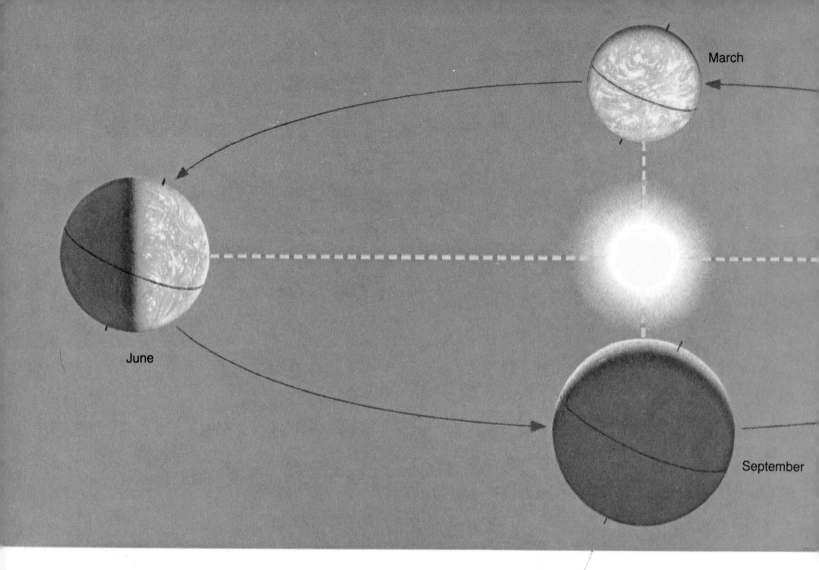

June

March

September

The Seasons

EARTH ROTATES AROUND its axis, an imaginary line that goes through the North and South poles. The axis is tilted 23.5 degrees. Earth has four seasons because it gets varying amounts of sunlight as it orbits the Sun. If its axis were straight up and down, Earth would get the same amount of sunlight each day and there would be no change of seasons.

About June 21 Earth's axis tilts most toward the Sun. Then the Sun shines directly on the northern part of the world. People there get more sunshine than on any other day. Above the Arctic Circle people have sunlight for 24 hours (the midnight Sun). Summer officially begins above the equator.

On the same day, sunlight hits the southern part of the world at a slant, delivering

less heat to each spot on the ground. People there get their smallest share of sunshine. Below the Antarctic Circle the Sun doesn't shine at all. Winter officially begins below the equator.

Six months later Earth's axis tilts most away from the Sun. About December 22 the seasons are reversed in the world. Winter starts in the northern half while summer starts in the southern half.

Twice a year, around March 21 and September 23, the Sun shines directly over the equator. All parts of the world have equal day and night. These days are called the equinoxes.

To get an idea of what a 23.5° angle looks like, hold your hand upright with the fingers spread apart. The angle between the ring and middle fingers is about 23.5°.

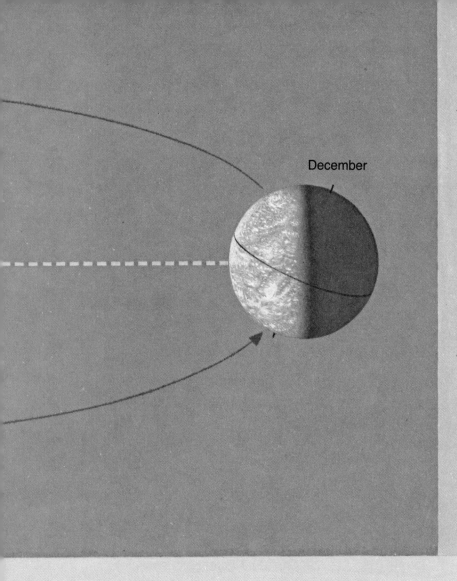

December

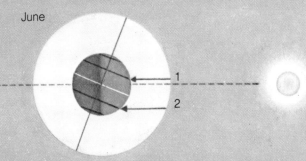

June

In summertime the Sun is high in the sky. Sunshine pours almost straight down to the ground. Because of this, sunshine is more concentrated in summer than in winter, when it hits at more of an angle. In the illustration above, the rays at region 1 hit Earth more directly than those at region 2 do. It is summertime north of the equator in June:

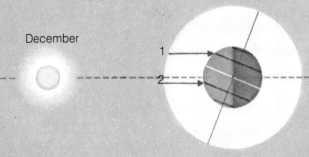

December

In December the rays hitting region 2 are more concentrated than the rays hitting region 1 are. The sunshine hitting region 1 is spread out over a greater area. It is summertime south of the equator in December.

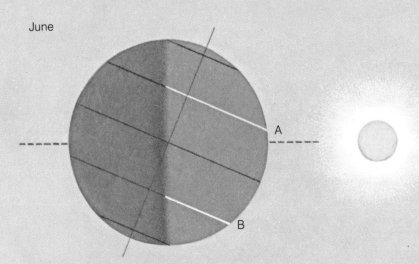

June

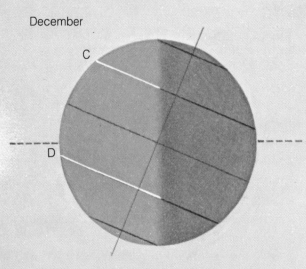

December

The above illustration shows the Northern Hemisphere during its summer when the North Pole is tilted toward the Sun and the South Pole is tilted away from the Sun. The Northern Hemisphere receives longer periods of sunlight than the Southern Hemisphere does. The Northern Hemisphere is having long days and short nights. In June a person at point A has a longer period of daylight than a person at point B does.

The illustration above shows the opposite situation. Now it is December and winter is beginning in the Northern Hemisphere. The North Pole is tilted away from the Sun, and the South Pole is tilted toward the Sun. The Northern Hemisphere is having short days and long nights. The Southern Hemisphere is having long days and short nights. Point D has a longer period of daylight than point C does.

Starlight

E NORMOUS DISTANCES PREVENT us from seeing the stars up close, even with a telescope. Luckily we can learn a lot about space by studying the starlight that comes to Earth.

Starlight is a mixture of several different forms of energy. The light that we can see with our eyes is only a small part of the electromagnetic radiation coming from space. We cannot see the ultraviolet, X, and gamma rays, which have much more energy than the visible light we can see. We also cannot see the infrared rays, which feel warm on our skin, and the radio waves like those that carry radio and television transmissions.

Each kind of star radiates a different mixture of visible and invisible light waves into space. The waves travel through space at the speed of light—over 186,000 miles (299,800 kilometers) per second. A light-year is the distance that light travels at this speed in one year. A light-year is almost 6 trillion miles (9.5 trillion kilometers).

Scientists collect starlight with telescopes. They separate it into patterns that give such information as what the star is made of and how hot it is.

Only some visible light, infrared and radio waves can get through the atmosphere and be collected by telescopes on Earth. So different telescopes are sent up in balloons, airplanes, rockets, and spacecraft to pick up all kinds of starlight before it is blocked by the atmosphere. Computers on Earth change information from invisible waves into pictures that show stars as never before seen by humans.

Our Sun is a star, and sunshine, like all starlight, is a mixture of colors. Here is an experiment that will show you the visible spectrum. Hold a prism so that a beam of sunlight passes through it. Move the prism until you see a rainbow of red, orange, yellow, green, blue, indigo, and violet spread out in a row. (Indigo may be difficult to see.)

All the colors of the spectrum travel through space together at the speed of light. They separate in materials such as glass and water because some slow down more than others. So when sunlight is passed through these materials, you see its colorful parts.

Water vapor in the air blocks infrared rays. Some infrared rays are gathered by telescopes located on high mountains; others, by detectors in airplanes, balloons, and rockets.

Stars can be seen best in a clear, dark sky. Giant telescopes are located high on mountains where the air overhead is thin, dry, and clean.

Many radio telescopes use a big curved surface to collect radio waves from space and then focus them on a large receiver. The Very Large Array in New Mexico has 27 antennas that can work together as one super-telescope.

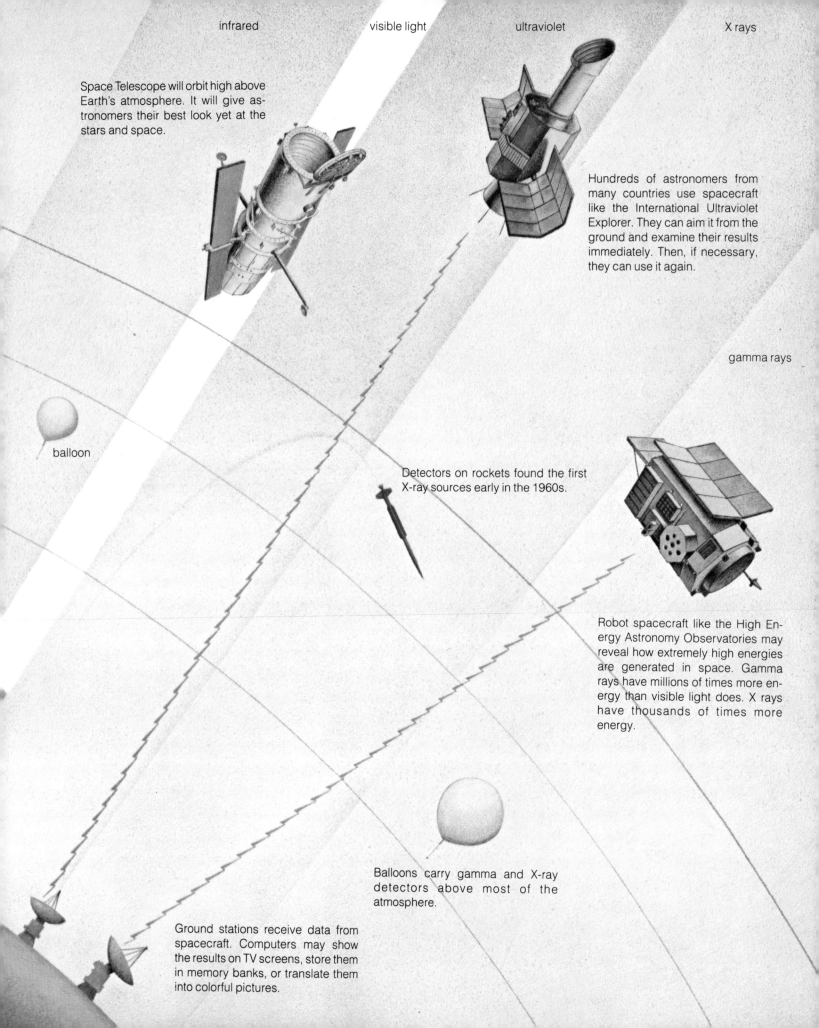

infrared   visible light   ultraviolet   X rays

Space Telescope will orbit high above Earth's atmosphere. It will give astronomers their best look yet at the stars and space.

Hundreds of astronomers from many countries use spacecraft like the International Ultraviolet Explorer. They can aim it from the ground and examine their results immediately. Then, if necessary, they can use it again.

gamma rays

balloon

Detectors on rockets found the first X-ray sources early in the 1960s.

Robot spacecraft like the High Energy Astronomy Observatories may reveal how extremely high energies are generated in space. Gamma rays have millions of times more energy than visible light does. X rays have thousands of times more energy.

Balloons carry gamma and X-ray detectors above most of the atmosphere.

Ground stations receive data from spacecraft. Computers may show the results on TV screens, store them in memory banks, or translate them into colorful pictures.

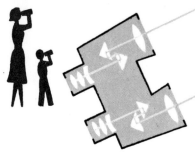

Binoculars collect more light than our eyes alone can collect. They are marked to give their power (magnification) and the size of their lenses. Binoculars labeled 7 x 50 are useful for stargazing (7 = power, 50 = millimeters of lens size).

Optical Telescopes

OUR EYES CAN SEE a few of the wonders of space, but we can see many more with a telescope. Even a small telescope can help us see distant stars and galaxies that are too faint to see with our eyes alone. The Moon and the planets look closer through a small telescope, and some of their features can be seen.

A telescope collects light from an object in the sky and forms its image. You can look at this image through a magnifying lens called an eyepiece. You can also record and analyze the image in other ways.

There are two basic types of telescopes: refractors and reflectors. A refracting telescope has a lens to gather the light and form an image. For stargazing, the lens is mounted at the front end of a tube that keeps out stray light. An eyepiece (lens) at the opposite end of the tube magnifies the image. The image is always inverted and reversed, or upside down and left to right.

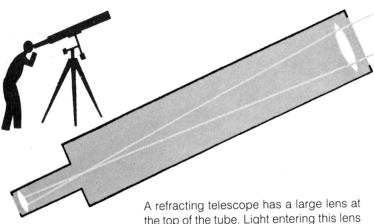

A refracting telescope has a large lens at the top of the tube. Light entering this lens is refracted, or bent, and forms an image near the bottom of the tube. With different eyepieces the magnifying power can be increased or decreased.

In a reflecting telescope a mirror produces images. For stargazing, it is mounted at the back end of a tube and reflects incoming light to form an image near the front end. A smaller mirror intercepts the light and reflects it to the eyepiece. Mirrors can be made very large to collect light from extremely faint objects. All the world's largest telescopes are reflectors.

The performance of a telescope depends a lot on the size and quality of its lens or mirror. The size of a telescope, such as a 6-inch (15-centimeter) or 200-inch (5-meter), refers to the main lens or the mirror. Here, bigger is better. A large mirror or lens shows sky objects brighter and clearer than a small one does.

You can use either a reflecting or a refracting telescope for your stargazing. A refractor is easier to care for, but a reflector of the same size is much less expensive. You can also make one yourself.

Astronomers rarely look through a giant telescope except to aim it. The light collected by the telescope is focused on electronic imaging systems and is then fed into instruments for analysis. The information may be recorded on photographic film, viewed on a television screen, or processed by a computer.

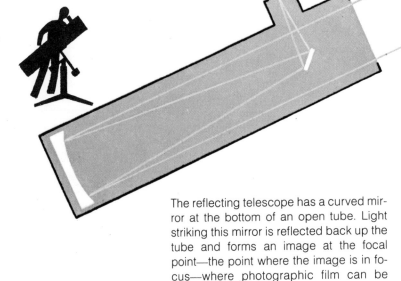

The reflecting telescope has a curved mirror at the bottom of an open tube. Light striking this mirror is reflected back up the tube and forms an image at the focal point—the point where the image is in focus—where photographic film can be placed.

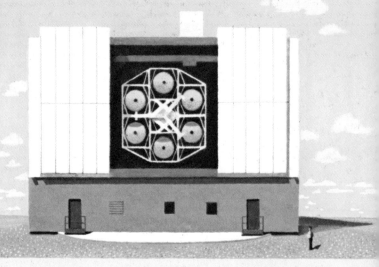

The largest American optical telescope is the 200-inch (5-meter) Hale reflector on Palomar Mountain in California, illustrated above. Motors move the heavy telescope into different viewing positions. The largest reflector in the world today is the 236-inch (6-meter) at the Special Astrophysical Observatory on Mount Pastukhov in the USSR. Construction began in Hawaii in 1985 on a 400-inch (10-meter) telescope.

The Multiple Mirror Telescope (MMT) atop Mount Hopkins, Arizona, is the world's third largest optical telescope. The six 72-inch (1.8-meter) reflectors perform like one huge 176-inch (4.5-meter) telescope. It is used for visible and infrared observations. Larger telescopes of the future may follow this type of low-cost multiple design.

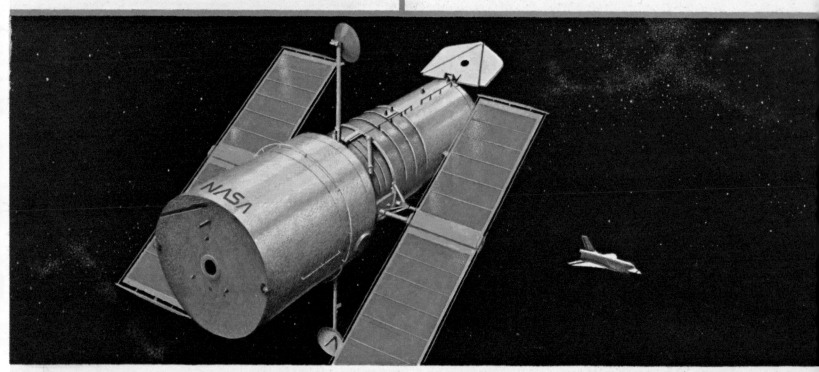

Our view of the universe will dramatically improve in this decade with Space Telescope. As it orbits above Earth's atmosphere the 96-inch (2.4-meter) mirror gives astronomers a much better view than any ever achieved on Earth. Space Telescope is remotely operated. Data is recorded and returned to the ground by radio. Astronauts from a space shuttle can make repairs and replace instrument packages for new experiments.

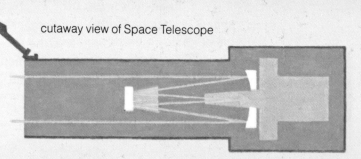

cutaway view of Space Telescope

Launch Vehicles

ROCKETS ARE USED TO send people and scientific instruments into space. They are useful for space travel because, unlike airplanes, they work in a vacuum.

All rockets work the same way as a deflating balloon in motion. When you blow up a balloon, you force air into it. The air presses outward in all directions. If you hold the neck closed, the air can't escape. The inflated balloon doesn't move. When you let go, air rushes out. Then the balloon zooms forward.

In a chemical rocket, fuel is burned to produce high-pressure hot gases. The hot gases race out the rear through an exhaust nozzle, creating forward thrust. While the fuel burns, the rocket is propelled forward. The fuel and the oxygen needed to burn it are called propellants.

Rockets like those used for colorful fireworks have solid propellants (a solid mixture of fuel plus a substance that releases oxygen). Solid fuel rockets cannot be easily shut off once they start burning.

A liquid fuel rocket engine can be controlled and shut off if necessary. Its propellants are stored separately. A fuel such as liquid hydrogen and an oxidizer such as liquid oxygen (lox) are used. A mixture of the propellants is fed into a combustion chamber for burning as needed.

Powerful launch vehicles often have two or three parts called stages. Each stage has its own engine and propellants. The first stage is used for liftoff. It must overcome Earth's gravity to lift a payload above the atmosphere. The upward thrust of the first stage has to be great enough to lift the full weight of the rocket plus payload off the ground. The upper stages do not need as large a thrust. They are used to reach orbital or interplanetary speeds. Each stage is jettisoned (discarded) when its propellants are used up.

Still more powerful rockets will be needed for future human space trips to the planets and beyond. Nuclear and electric rocket motors may provide the higher thrusts and velocities needed.

Saturn V Apollo (USA)

COMPARATIVE SIZES OF SOME LAUNCH VEHICLES AND PAYLOADS.

Juno 1 (USA)

Vanguard (USA)

A-1 Sputnik (USSR)

A-1 Vostok (USSR)

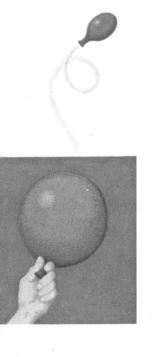

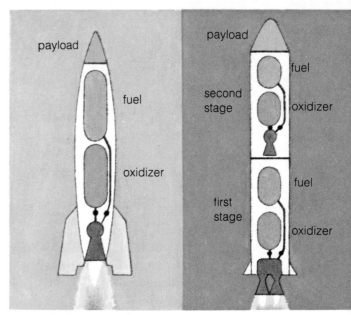

payload

single stage rocket

fuel

oxidizer

payload

second stage

fuel

oxidizer

first stage

fuel

oxidizer

multistage rocket

If you inflate a balloon and then release it (left), the air flowing out creates a forward thrust that pushes the balloon ahead. The fuel and oxidizer of the single-stage rocket (right) burn in the combustion chamber, and the escaping gas thrusts the rocket forward. The first stage of the multistage rocket (far right) is used for the liftoff that overcomes Earth's gravity. After the first stage is jettisoned, the second stage is used to reach orbital speed.

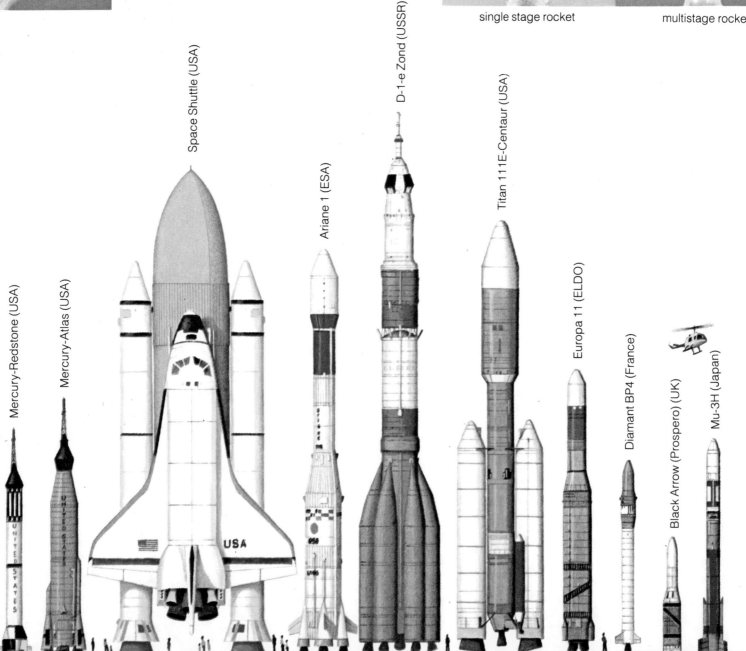

Mercury-Redstone (USA)

Mercury-Atlas (USA)

Space Shuttle (USA)

Ariane 1 (ESA)

D-1-e Zond (USSR)

Titan 111E-Centaur (USA)

Europa 11 (ELDO)

Diamant BP4 (France)

Black Arrow (Prospero) (UK)

Mu-3H (Japan)

Satellites and Probes

SPACECRAFT THAT ORBIT Earth are launched by rockets. These spacecraft are called satellites, and their orbits are usually ellipses. The point of an orbit closest to Earth is called the perigee; the most distant point is called the apogee. A combination of their forward velocity and Earth's gravity keeps these satellites in orbit.

Most satellites are launched from west to east because the least amount of rocket energy is needed. Earth's rotation from west to east boosts the rocket.

Launching a satellite into a polar orbit, which takes it over the North and South poles, requires more rocket energy because Earth's rotation doesn't help. This orbit is used for some weather satellites and some resource satellites that aid in pollution control, the search for oil, and the mapping of Earth's surface.

As a satellite goes around Earth it can photograph a strip of Earth with each pass. Because Earth rotates below the satellite, a different strip is photographed with each orbit. After a number of days the satellite has photographed the entire surface of Earth.

Communications satellites are usually placed in a synchronous orbit above Earth's equator. They complete one orbit in exactly the same time Earth turns once on its axis. So these satellites are always over the same point on Earth.

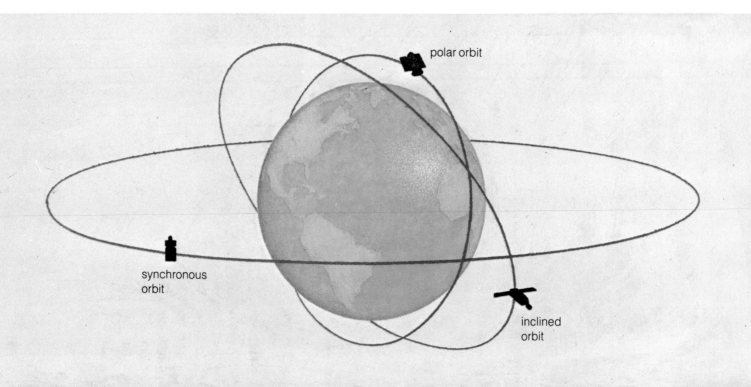

Satellites in a polar orbit (above) travel over the North and South poles, and those in an inclined orbit travel at an angle to the equator. In a synchronous orbit a satellite makes one orbit in exactly the same time that Earth turns once on its axis. A satellite in this kind of orbit stays over the same point on Earth at all times.

In a circular orbit (right) a satellite travels at a constant speed at a constant distance from Earth. Most orbits are elliptical. At perigee the satellite is closest to Earth and goes fastest. At apogee it is farthest from Earth and travels slowest.

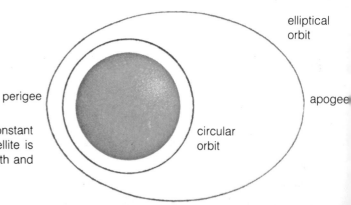

Because many different types of satellites are placed in synchronous orbits, this orbital space is getting quite crowded. Most of the world's long-distance telephone calls are placed through communications satellites in synchronous orbits. These satellites are also used to relay television programs.

Satellites cannot stay in orbit around Earth forever. Depending on its size and its orbital distance from Earth, a satellite may stay up for a few years or several hundred years. As a satellite orbits Earth the drag of Earth's atmosphere eventually slows it down. Ultimately the orbital speed slows so much that gravity pulls the satellite back to Earth. Friction causes most satellites to burn up as they plunge through the atmosphere.

Space probes that escape Earth's gravity and travel to other planets are also launched by rockets. Then, except for mid-course corrections, they coast under the pull of gravity of the Sun and nearby massive objects.

Scientists must take into account the positions of Earth and the target planet both on the day of launch and afterward. The probe must be launched with just the right velocity so that gravity pulls it along a course that meets the moving planet. Since many planetary probes take years to reach their targets, extremely precise calculations must be made far in advance of an actual encounter.

When scientists plotted the course of probes and manned missions to the Moon, they had to make very exact calculations. Since the Moon orbits Earth, scientists had to aim the craft at launch so that it would meet the moving Moon. Calculations had to be precise to land a craft on a target that also spins on its axis. Computers have made it possible to do complex calculations like these quickly.

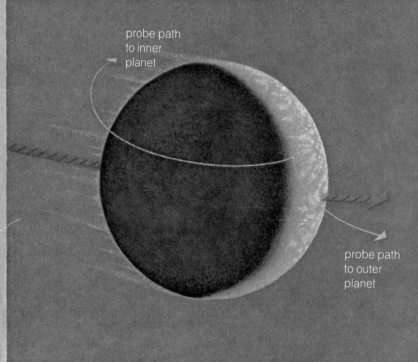

A probe to a planet that is farther away from the Sun than Earth is must be launched at a greater speed than that of Earth moving around the Sun. The launch is made from west to east to give the probe an extra boost. A probe to a planet closer to the Sun must be launched so that its initial speed is slower than Earth's. The probe is launched in a direction opposite to Earth's motion around the Sun.

The Solar System

THE SUN AND ALL the objects that orbit it—including Earth—form the solar system. The Sun is the largest, heaviest, and hottest body in our solar system. It is also the source of all the system's light and heat.

The only star in our solar system, the Sun controls all of the other bodies around it. Even tiny Pluto—whose orbit is some 4 billion miles away—is governed by the Sun.

Each of the nine known planets in the solar system has two motions. Every planet rotates, or spins, on its own axis. At the same time it also revolves around the Sun.

The time required for one complete rotation is called a day. Our day is 24 hours long. Jupiter's day is the shortest—under 10 hours. Venus is the slowest of the planets in its rotation, a single rotation taking 243 of our days.

The time required for a planet to make one complete

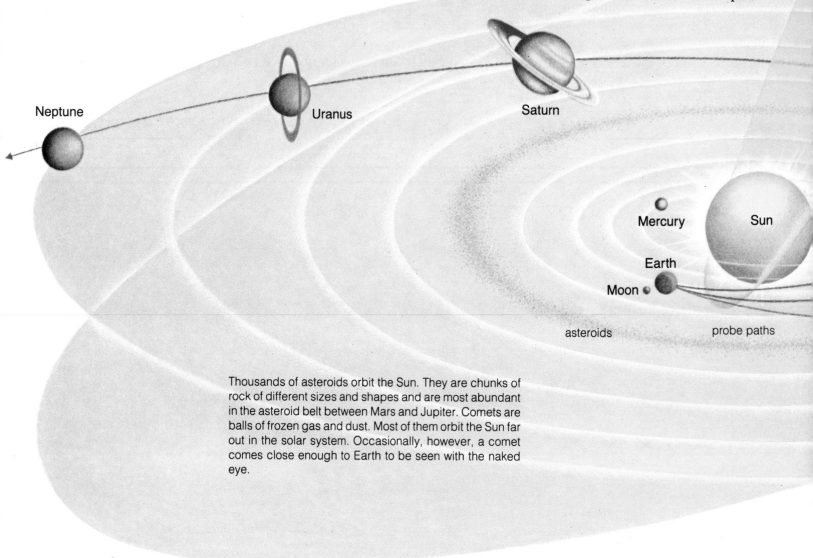

Neptune · Uranus · Saturn · Mercury · Sun · Earth · Moon · asteroids · probe paths

Thousands of asteroids orbit the Sun. They are chunks of rock of different sizes and shapes and are most abundant in the asteroid belt between Mars and Jupiter. Comets are balls of frozen gas and dust. Most of them orbit the Sun far out in the solar system. Occasionally, however, a comet comes close enough to Earth to be seen with the naked eye.

revolution around the Sun is called a year. A year on Earth is 365 ¼ days. Planets closer to the Sun have shorter years. A year on Mercury is the shortest—only 88 of our days. A year on Pluto is longest, equal to 247 of our years.

All of the planets except Mercury and Venus have moons. The largest is Ganymede, a moon that orbits Jupiter. Jupiter, Saturn, Uranus, and probably Neptune are circled by rings.

There are countless smaller bodies that belong to the solar system. Among them are asteroids, which are minor planets; comets, which are frozen balls of gases; and meteoroids, which are solid particles.

Mercury, Venus, Mars, Jupiter, and Saturn look like stars in the sky. People observed that these bodies moved among the real stars. They called these moving bodies "planets," which comes from the Greek word meaning "wanderers."

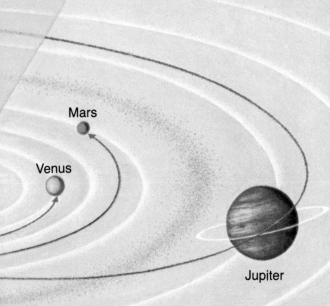

comet

Mars

Venus

Jupiter

Scientists think that the solar system began as a gigantic whirling space cloud that slowly collapsed and flattened out some 5 billion years ago. Most of the dust and gas forming the cloud centered in a huge fiery ball that became the Sun. Smaller clumps piled up away from the center, forming the planets and their moons. All of these objects still move like the original cloud.

Pluto

The whole solar system moves through space.

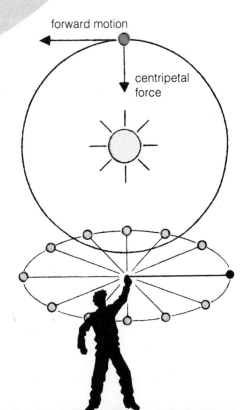

forward motion

centripetal force

The illustration at the right explains how planets are forced to orbit the Sun. At the top a planet is shown in orbit. The arrows indicate the planet's forward motion and the centripetal (inward) force operating on it. At the bottom a ball on the end of a string is orbiting the boy who is whirling it. The same effect is at work here. The moving ball stays in orbit because the string exerts an inward force on it. The force on the planet, which acts like a giant invisible string (the arrow pointing toward the Sun), is called gravity. All objects in the solar system attract each other with this force. The combination of the planets' forward motion and the inward pull of the Sun's gravity forces the planets to follow their orbits instead of flying straight out into space.

The giant planets—Jupiter, Saturn, Uranus, and Neptune—are much bigger than Earth. All have more mass than our planet, but they are not as dense. These planets are made mostly of the light gases hydrogen and helium. They each have many moons.

Jupiter

Mars

Earth

Moon

Venus

Mercury

The Sun is much bigger and heavier than all of the planets. It takes up over 900 times more space than Jupiter and has 740 times more mass than all of the planets together.

The smaller terrestrial planets—Mercury, Venus, Earth, and Mars—are closest to the Sun. All have a high density and must have rocks and metals inside. Only Earth has abundant water and living things. These planets have few moons. Earth has one, Mars has two, and Mercury and Venus have none.

Mysterious Pluto is still a question mark. It does not really fit into either the terrestrial or the giant group of planets. Pluto orbits farthest away from the Sun but seems to be small and rocky. It has one moon. Because Pluto goes inside the orbit of Neptune, some people think it is not a planet at all. It could be an escaped moon of Neptune.

Saturn

Uranus

Pluto

Neptune

The Planets

Sun

ALL THE PLANETS except Mercury and Pluto are covered by an atmosphere. The colors of these atmospheres come from their makeup. Earth's white clouds are made of water vapor. Sulfur gives the clouds of Venus their yellow color. Jupiter's brilliant bands are still a mystery.

The biggest planet is Jupiter. Earth measures 7,930 miles (12,756 kilometers) across. Over 1,300 Earths would fit inside Jupiter. Jupiter also has the most mass of all the planets. Mass is the amount of matter inside an object. Jupiter's mass is 318 times Earth's.

The density of an object tells how much mass is packed inside and is also a clue to what makes up the mass. Water is used for comparisons. Solids, such as rock and iron, have a higher density than water. Gases have a lower density. Mercury, the smallest and lightest planet, is relatively dense, so it must be rocky and probably has an iron core.

25

The Sun

COMPARED TO OTHER stars in the universe, our Sun is quite ordinary. It is not any larger, hotter, or brighter than many of the stars that you see as tiny points of light. The reason the Sun is more impressive is that it is much closer to us—only about 93 million miles (143 million kilometers) away. The next closest star is practically 300,000 times farther away.

The Sun is a tremendous ball of hot, glowing gases. It is bigger than a million Earths in volume. Its surface temperature is about 10,000° F. (5,530° C.). Deep inside its temperature is probably 25 million degrees F. (15 million degrees C.).

Hydrogen and helium are the main ingredients of the Sun. It also contains at least sixty other elements that are found on Earth. Hydrogen is the Sun's fuel. Every second about 5 million tons of hydrogen in the Sun's core change into helium, releasing great amounts of energy. The process is called nuclear fusion.

The released energy rises to the surface after many years and radiates into space. This solar energy is our sunshine. Only a small part of the Sun's total radiation reaches Earth. Its travel time from the Sun is 8 ⅓ minutes.

Without the Sun's energy human beings would not exist on Earth. However, long and direct exposure to the Sun's high-energy gamma, X, and ultraviolet rays could kill all living things. Our atmosphere screens out most of these rays before they reach the ground.

Pictures taken through telescopes show that the Sun is always changing. Bright spots, called granules, show up like grains of rice on its surface. They are the tops of gas currents from the hotter interior.

Sunspots appear for a few hours or for months. They are cooler than the surrounding gases, so they look like dark patches. A sunspot can be as big as Earth, and many of them are larger than that.

On a particular day there may be a hundred sunspots—or none at all. A maximum number of sunspots appear approximately every 11 years. They are related to the magnetic field of the Sun. Sometimes powerful magnetic forces cause great storms nearby. Sudden gigantic explosions, called flares, hurl bursts of radiation and material outward. Soon after this happens, their effects can be seen and heard on Earth.

Electrified gases from the Sun strike our air mainly near the North and South poles, causing the aurora borealis (northern lights) and the aurora australis (southern lights). These blasts of electrified gas can cause TV and radio transmission difficulties and electrical surges on power lines.

The solar wind, a flow of electrified gases, streams outward from the Sun. It spouts in regions called coronal holes. Big blasts of wind come from violent flares.

Scientists monitor the Sun every day. They hope to learn what makes its energy output change. The Solar Maximum Year in 1980–1981 was the biggest Sun-watch program so far. Hundreds of scientists in eighteen countries monitored the Sun. As a result more data was gathered on the Sun's activity than ever before in history.

The McMath Solar Telescope on Kitt Peak in Arizona is the world's largest Sun telescope. It tracks the Sun during the day. A 60-inch (1.5-meter) mirror at the top of the tower catches sunlight (1) and sends it underground (2). Another mirror (3) beams the light to an observing room (4).

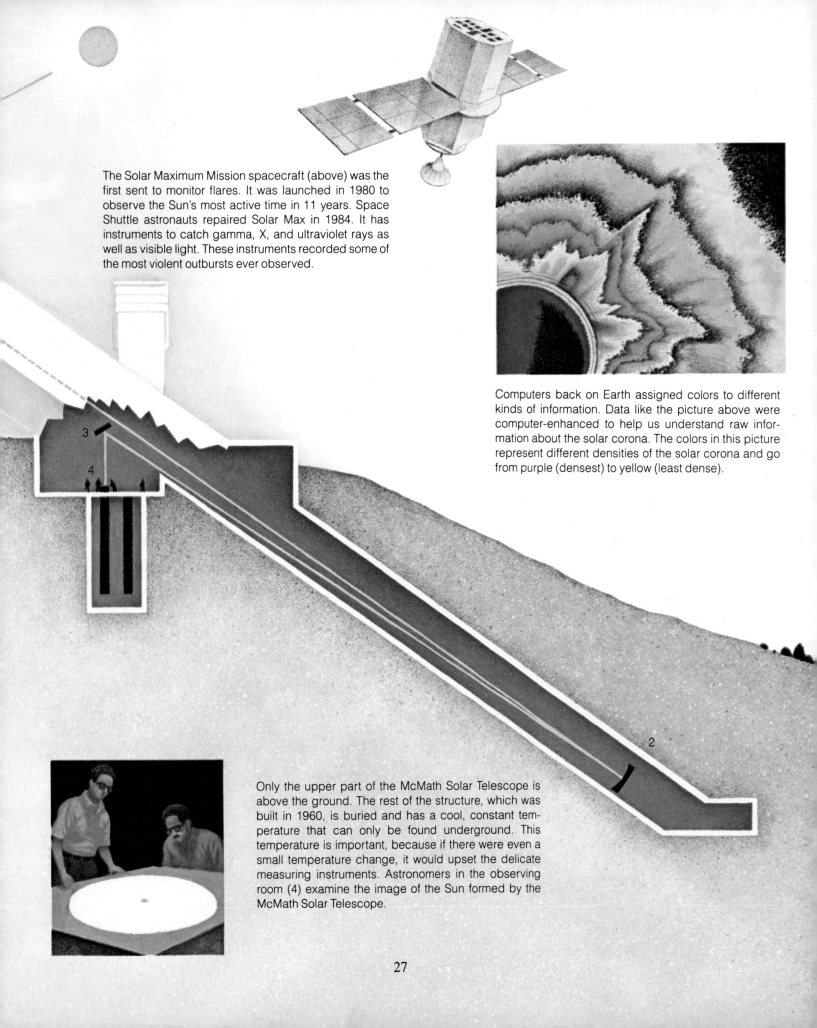

The Solar Maximum Mission spacecraft (above) was the first sent to monitor flares. It was launched in 1980 to observe the Sun's most active time in 11 years. Space Shuttle astronauts repaired Solar Max in 1984. It has instruments to catch gamma, X, and ultraviolet rays as well as visible light. These instruments recorded some of the most violent outbursts ever observed.

Computers back on Earth assigned colors to different kinds of information. Data like the picture above were computer-enhanced to help us understand raw information about the solar corona. The colors in this picture represent different densities of the solar corona and go from purple (densest) to yellow (least dense).

Only the upper part of the McMath Solar Telescope is above the ground. The rest of the structure, which was built in 1960, is buried and has a cool, constant temperature that can only be found underground. This temperature is important, because if there were even a small temperature change, it would upset the delicate measuring instruments. Astronomers in the observing room (4) examine the image of the Sun formed by the McMath Solar Telescope.

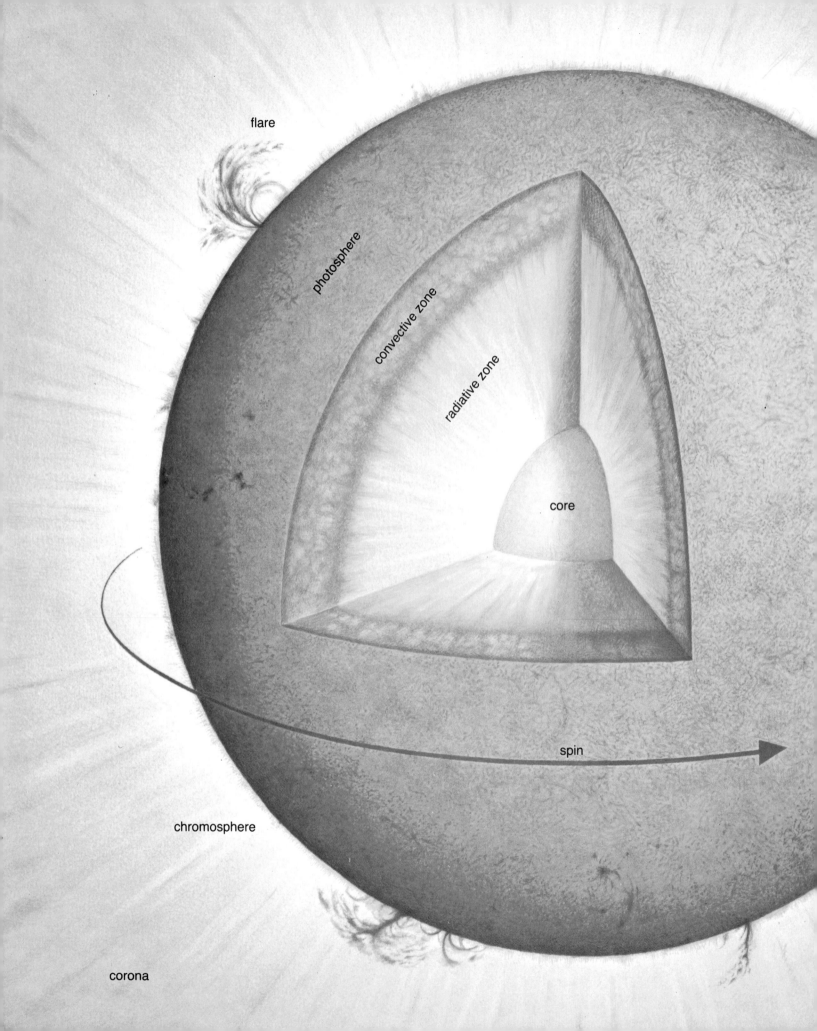

flare

photosphere

convective zone

radiative zone

core

spin

chromosphere

corona

prominence

sunspot

Our Closest Star

I N THE CORE DEEP inside the Sun, heat and light are produced. The energy from the superhot core flows up through the radiative zone. Finally streams of gas take the energy to the surface and then they sink again in the zone of convection.

The part of the sun that is visible to us is called the photosphere. This is a hot, thin layer of gas that radiates sunshine.

The chromosphere is the Sun's lower atmosphere. It extends a few thousand miles above the photosphere.

The corona is the Sun's outer atmosphere. It extends millions of miles into space and consists of a very thin, very hot gas. The temperature of the corona is about 3.5 million degrees F. (2 million degrees C.).

Sunspots are cooler, and therefore darker, patches that sometimes appear on the bright part of the Sun. A prominence is a blazing burst of gas. Sometimes a prominence shoots up hundreds of thousands of miles and then loops back down. A solar flare is a gigantic explosion that hurls large amounts of radiation and material into space.

The Sun spins on its own axis, but not in the same way as our solid Earth does. Gases in the middle rotate faster than those at the top and bottom do.

The Sun and all stars send out clues about their composition. Stars give off a continuous spectrum of visible light. When this light passes through the gases of the star's atmosphere, some is absorbed. This absorption shows up on the recorded spectrum as dark lines. There is a special pattern for each chemical element. This information tells scientists what elements make up the star. Study of these lines can also reveal information about the star's temperature and motion.

SUN

Average distance from Earth:
93,000,000 miles
150,000,000 kilometers

Diameter at equator:
864,000 miles
1,392,000 kilometers

Surface temperature:
10,000°F

Spins on axis in:
equator: 25 days
poles: 35 days

Average density:
1.4 (water = 1)

 A person who weighs 100 pounds on Earth would weigh 2,800 pounds on the Sun.

WARNING: NEVER look straight at the Sun, especially with binoculars or a telescope. You could permanently injure your eyes or blind yourself if you do. Project the image of the Sun onto a white card as shown.

A meteorite crashes into Mercury's surface.

Mercury

MERCURY IS A SMALL planet, not even half as big as Earth. Its gravity is much weaker too. A person weighing 100 pounds (45 kilograms) on Earth would weigh only 38 pounds (17 kilograms) on Mercury.

Only 36 million miles (58 kilometers) from the Sun—closer than any other planet—Mercury makes one complete orbit about every three months. The fastest of all the planets, it travels at about 108,000 miles per hour (48 kilometers per second). It was named for the Roman messenger of the gods.

Dust covers the surface of this waterless, lifeless planet. Mercury suffers extremes of heat and cold, since it has hardly any protective atmosphere. When the Sun is overhead, the planet's temperature soars to 800° F. (426° C.). This is about seven times higher than the hottest deserts on Earth. At midnight the temperature falls to −300° F. (−180° C.).

The density of Mercury is about the same as Earth's, and it probably has an iron core.

Many craters scar Mercury's surface. Caloris Basin, the largest, measures 930 miles (1,300 kilo-

The craters on Mercury were most likely blasted by meteorites that crashed into the planet billions of years ago (left). Some craters have "rays" radiating from the center. Bouncing fragments can make smaller craters ringing the larger one (above).

Our best look at Mercury was provided by Mariner 10 in 1974 and 1975. It took 3,000 pictures of the planet and measured its temperature, ground makeup, and the solar wind. All of this information was radioed back to Earth.

MERCURY

The diameter of Mercury is slightly more than .33 that of Earth.

Position from Sun: first planet

Average distance from Sun:
36,000,000 miles
57,900,000 kilometers

Diameter at equator:
3,030 miles
4,880 kilometers

Orbits Sun in:
88 days

Spins on axis in:
59 days

Density: 5.4 (water = 1)

 A person who weighs 100 pounds on Earth would weigh 38 pounds on Mercury.

Known satellites:
None

IN THE SKY: Mercury is hard to spot. It is quite small and close to the bright Sun. The best times to observe Mercury are when it is farthest from the Sun. Then it looks like a star in the west at sunset or a star in the east at sunrise.

THROUGH A TELESCOPE: Mercury looks like a blob of light without features. You can see its shape change.

meters) across. This is wider than the state of Alaska. Most likely a chunk of rock from space crashed there. The force of the collision that formed the basin thrust up huge mountains. Flying debris cut out long, grooved valleys.

Some of Mercury's craters are filled with lava. The lava may have come from volcanoes or from rocks melted by the mighty crashes of meteorites. Some of the craters are separated from each other by broad lava plains. Long lines of cliffs, called scarps, cross the plains.

Because it is so small and so close to the Sun, Mercury is difficult to see. The best times to observe it are when it is farthest from the Sun. Then it looks like a ''star'' in the western sky at sunset or a ''morning star'' in the eastern sky at sunrise.

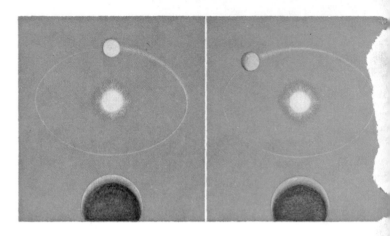

Every 19 months Venus is directly opposite Earth on the far side of the Sun. Then it is at its farthest point from Earth (left, above). Its fully lighted side is facing us, but the Sun blocks our view. As Venus proceeds in its orbit (above, right), half of it is in sunlight, but an edge facing us is not receiving sunlight, so it looks dark.

Venus

FOR CENTURIES PEOPLE believed that Venus was inhabited. Now we know that this is impossible. No life as we know it could survive on the planet. Even the robot spacecraft that have been sent there cannot function on Venus for more than a couple of hours. Venus is about the same size and density as Earth and has about the same gravity. But Venus is completely hostile to life.

Pale yellow clouds cover Venus, completely hiding its surface from view. The clouds consist mostly of droplets of sulfuric acid. The heavy atmosphere of this planet is about 97 percent carbon dioxide, compared to .03 percent on Earth. The atmospheric pressure is 1,330 pounds per square inch, over 90 times greater than that on Earth.

The temperature on Venus is nearly 900° F. (470° C.)— more than four times higher than the temperature of boiling water on Earth. The carbon dioxide and water vapor in the air on Venus let in sunlight, but they trap the heat and do not let it out. Because of this "greenhouse effect" the planet gets hotter and hotter.

Days go by slowly on Venus, which has the slowest rotation of all the planets. Venus orbits the Sun in the same direction as Earth, but it rotates in the opposite direction. So on Venus the Sun "rises" in the west and "sets" in the east. Because Venus rotates slowly in a direction opposite to the way it circles the sun, a single day lasts 117 of our days.

There is thunder and lightning in the grim atmosphere of Venus, the second planet from the Sun.

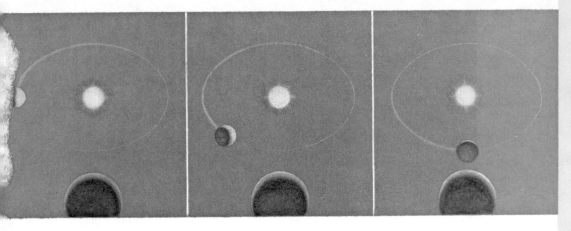

When Venus has completed one fourth of its orbit (above, left) the part we see is half in light and half in darkness, so it looks like a half moon. At this point the part we see lighted looks brighter because it is closer to Earth. As it comes nearer Earth (above, center) it looks like a crescent. Finally, halfway around its orbit (above, right), Venus has reached the point where it is closest to Earth. Its lighted side faces directly away from us. This illustration shows Venus 9½ months after the illustration at the far left of the opposite page. Venus is now only 26 million miles (42 million kilometers) from Earth, and it is between Earth and the Sun.

Venus is the easiest planet to see in the sky and shines more brightly at night than anything except the Moon. It has attracted the attention of sky observers since the earliest times. There are even references to Venus on very old stone tablets. The Romans named the planet after their goddess of love and beauty. The ancients called Venus the Morning Star when it sparkled brightly in the east just before sunrise. When it glittered in the west just after sunset, they called it the Evening Star.

With a telescope or binoculars you can see Venus change in shape and brightness. It goes through phases like the Moon does. Venus circles the Sun every 225 days inside Earth's orbit, so we see it from different positions.

So far Venus has been explored by 21 spacecraft. Sixteen of the robot explorers were Russian, and 5 were American. Each radioed its information to Earth, and none returned.

In 1966 the Soviet Venera 3 landed on Venus but was quickly crushed by the heavy atmosphere and did not return any data to Earth. In 1975 Venera 9 and Venera 10 landed on Venus and took the first photographs of the dry, rocky planet. At the end of 1978 the American Pioneer Venus 1 arrived and began to orbit the planet. It took cloud pictures and made weather reports and radar measurements. Venera 13 and 14 landed and took the first color television pictures of Venus in 1982. In 1984 orbiters Venera 15 and 16 imaged the planet, using radar. Within two hours after landing, all robot spacecraft were out of operation in the extreme conditions of this hostile planet.

These explorations have provided the data that gives us our present knowledge of Venus. More than half of the planet is relatively flat land with apparent craters. There are some dry basins. Highlands appear like our continents, one of them about the size of Australia. Maxwell Montes, the highest point, is nearly 7 miles (11 kilometers) high—higher than Mount Everest.

VENUS

The diameter of Venus is .95 that of Earth.

Position from Sun: second planet

Average distance from Sun:
67,000,000 miles
108,200,000 kilometers

Diameter at equator:
7,520 miles
12,100 kilometers

Orbits Sun in:
225 days

Spins on axis in:
243 days

Density: 5.3 (water = 1)

 A person who weighs 100 pounds on Earth would weigh 91 pounds on Venus.

Known satellites:
None

IN THE SKY: Venus is the easiest planet to spot. It shines more brightly than everything in the sky except the Sun and the Moon. Venus is dazzling because it is covered by clouds that reflect a lot of sunlight. Sometimes it is so bright that it is mistaken for an unidentified flying object (UFO).

THROUGH A TELESCOPE: You can see the shape and brightness of Venus change. Venus goes through phases like the Moon does. It circles the Sun every 225 days inside Earth's orbit, so we see it from different positions.

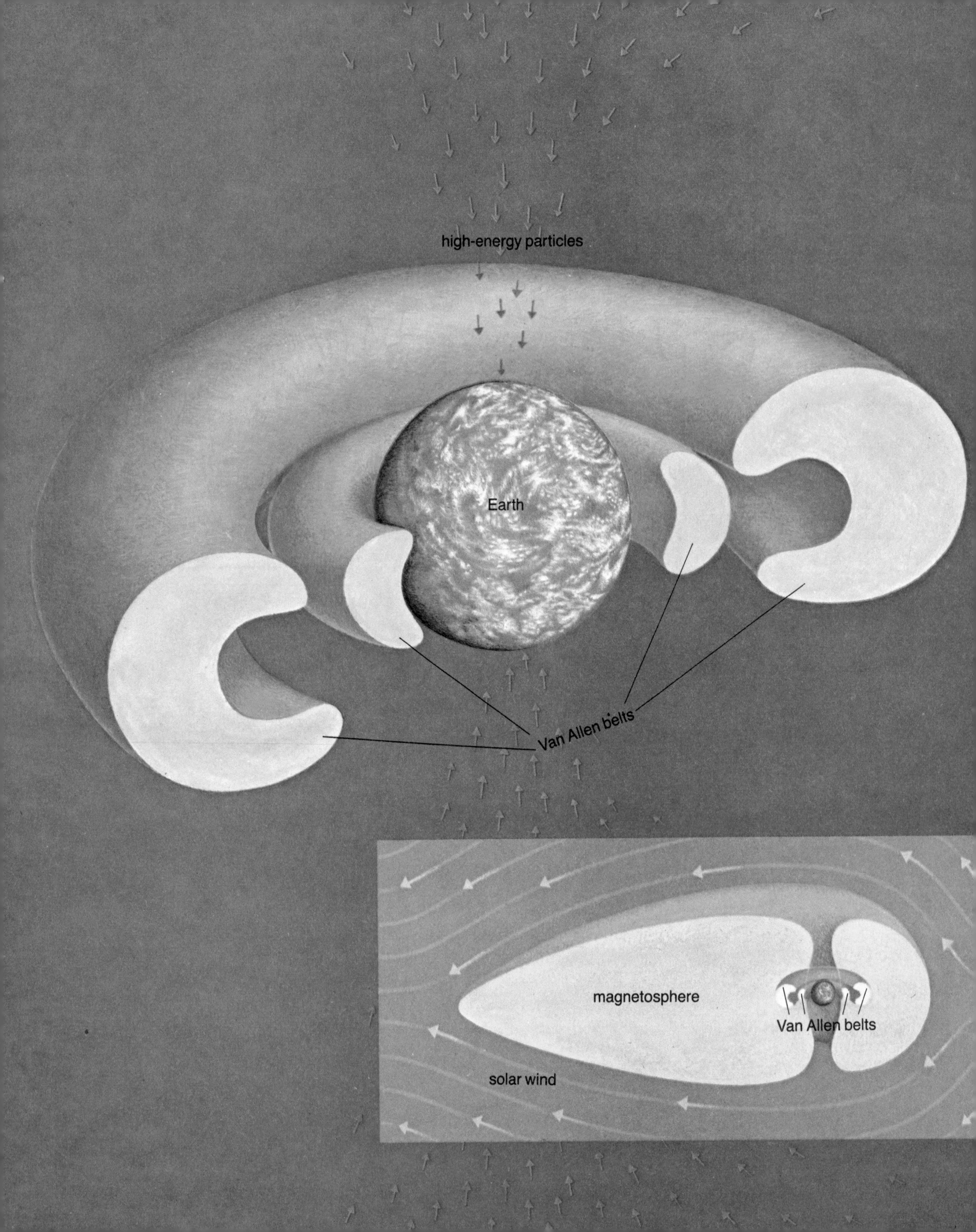

high-energy particles

Earth

Van Allen belts

magnetosphere

Van Allen belts

solar wind

Planet Earth

EARTH RESEMBLES THE other planets in many ways, but it is very special. It is the only planet that we know of that supports life.

Animals and plants, as we know them, need energy, warmth, water, and air. Earth provides these needs. Located about 93 million miles (149.6 million kilometers) from the Sun, it gets enough sunshine to support life. Temperatures are comfortable in most places all year long.

No other planet is known to have flowing water on its surface. More than 70 percent of Earth's total surface area of 198 million square miles (510 million square kilometers) is covered by water.

Our planet weighs about 6,600 million trillion tons. Its mass creates a force of gravity that pulls everything toward the center of the planet. Earth's gravity is powerful enough to hold a huge mass of air close to its surface.

Most likely Earth formed with the other planets and the Sun about 5 billion years ago. At first its air was poisonous and there was no life. Over billions of years Earth has changed.

From a gas mixture of methane, ammonia, and carbon dioxide, and water vapor in the early atmosphere, sparked by lightning and the Sun's radiation, could have come the first organic molecules—the building blocks of all Earth life. No one knows precisely when the first living things appeared on Earth, but fossil records in ancient rocks show that one-celled plants and animals were here 3 billion years ago.

Today Earth continues to change. Water and winds work on the surface, tearing it down in some places and building it up in others. Volcanoes and earthquakes alter it from below the surface.

The only way we can learn how Earth is built is from measurements made on the surface. We picture it in the following parts:

The core, about 2,170 miles (3,470 kilometers) thick, is probably made of iron and nickel. It seems to have a solid center surrounded by a liquid layer. The temperature is about 11,000° F. (6,100° C.), similar to the surface of the Sun.

The mantle, about 1,800 miles (2,880 kilometers) thick, is hot, dense rock. The mantle will give or bend under a steady force but breaks if it is hit hard.

The crust, an average of 22 miles (35 kilometers) thick, is made of lightweight rocks such as granite and basalt. The continents and oceans are here.

The atmosphere surrounds the whole planet. Earth is not perfectly round. It bulges slightly at the equator. The distance across Earth at the equator is more than 26 miles (42.5 kilometers) greater than the distance across the poles. This bulge is probably the result of rotation over the past 5 billion years.

Earth reflects sunlight as the other planets do. From the Moon it can be seen shining in the sky. It looks colorful, with white clouds, blue oceans, red-brown continents, and white ice at the North and South poles.

The magnetosphere is the region around Earth where magnetic forces work (left, inset). Earth acts like a giant magnet, and its magnetic force is powerful thousands of miles out in space. At large distances from Earth the solar wind gives the magnetosphere its teardrop shape. Within the magnetosphere the Van Allen belts circle Earth like two huge doughnuts. Here the magnetic forces are so strong that they trap many electrical particles in the solar wind. If these particles were to strike us, they could kill us. Instead they spin around inside the Van Allen belts. During heavy solar activity enough of the particles get through to Earth's atmosphere, especially near the magnetic poles, to cause bright bands of light called auroras.

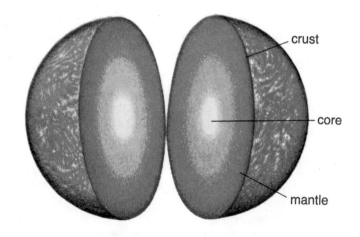

Drifting Continents

OUR EARTH KEEPS CHANGING. Although it was formed almost 5 billion years ago, the oldest rocks around date back only 3.6 billion years. Water and wind wear down the planet from the outside. Volcanoes, mountain building, and earthquakes also shape the planet.

Scientists say that the continents ride on huge slabs of rock. These rock slabs are called plates. Volcanic eruptions, earthquakes, and some forms of mountain building occur in those places where one huge rock slab pushes into or rides over another.

The plates move constantly but slowly. Every year the continents move a bit in relation to each other; but an inch (2.5 centimeters) per year over 200 million years adds up to 3,000 miles (4,800 kilometers).

Young rocks are found in the middle of the ocean, as at the Mid-Atlantic Ridge, where plates are separating. Here material flows out from inside Earth and hardens, sometimes forming a long chain of mountains on the ocean bottom.

Millions of years ago the world looked very different than it does today. Antarctica, the region around the South Pole, was located in a warm spot far away from where it is now. South America was connected to Africa. North America was connected to Europe. The drifting continents changed Earth's geography.

Today the Atlantic Ocean separates South America from Africa. But the eastern coastline of South America would fit snugly into the western coastline of Africa like a piece in a jigsaw puzzle. Both continents have the same kinds of fossil plant and animal life along their coastlines, which is another indication that they were once joined.

The rocks near the coasts of South America and Africa are 150 million years old. Those in the middle of the Atlantic Ocean are younger, giving us more evidence that these continents were once joined.

Alfred Wegener (1880–1930), a German geologist, meteorologist, and explorer, suggested the idea of continental drift in the first half of this century. Evidence to support the continental drift theory, also called the theory of plate tectonics, has been accumulating since the second half of this century.

What powers the continental drift? The most popular theory says that streams of warm rock move up from inside Earth. When they hit the cold, rigid rocks

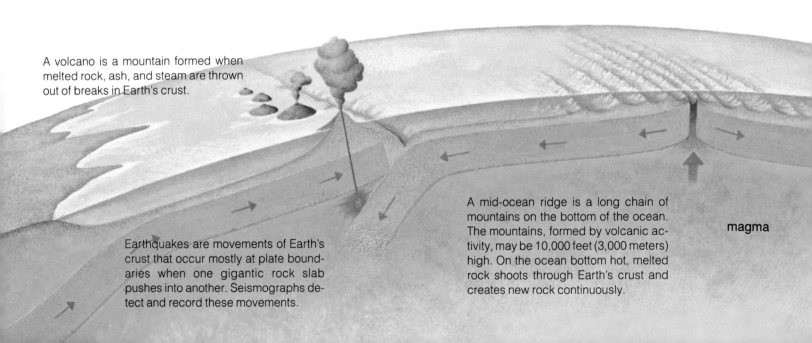

A volcano is a mountain formed when melted rock, ash, and steam are thrown out of breaks in Earth's crust.

Earthquakes are movements of Earth's crust that occur mostly at plate boundaries when one gigantic rock slab pushes into another. Seismographs detect and record these movements.

A mid-ocean ridge is a long chain of mountains on the bottom of the ocean. The mountains, formed by volcanic activity, may be 10,000 feet (3,000 meters) high. On the ocean bottom hot, melted rock shoots through Earth's crust and creates new rock continuously.

magma

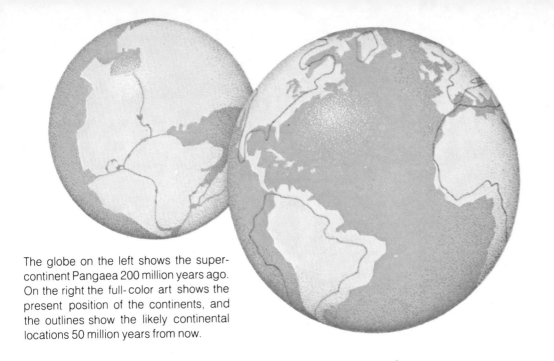

The globe on the left shows the super-continent Pangaea 200 million years ago. On the right the full-color art shows the present position of the continents, and the outlines show the likely continental locations 50 million years from now.

above, they divide into two separate streams. These streams then move in opposite directions and finally sink again. The plates carrying the continents are dragged along by the moving rock streams.

About 200 million years ago there was one supercontinent on Earth that we call Pangaea, which means "all land." It was surrounded by the ocean. At that time it was probably beginning to break up into sections that looked something like the continents of today.

Our continents on huge rock slabs are still drifting. Earthquakes, volcanoes, mountain building, and breaks in Earth's crust occur mostly at the boundaries between these rock slabs, or plates. Millions of years from now, if the plates keep moving, the Atlantic Ocean will be wider, the Mediterranean Sea will close, and Australia will meet Eurasia. In 10 million years Los Angeles, located on the Pacific plate, will meet San Francisco, located on the North American plate.

Mountain ranges, such as the Rockies and the Alps, are created at plate boundaries where gigantic rock slabs collide and buckle Earth's crust.

EARTH

Position from Sun: third planet

Average distance from Sun:
93,000,000 miles
149,600,000 kilometers

Diameter at equator:
7,930 miles
12,756 kilometers

Orbits Sun in:
1 year

Spins on axis in:
23 hours, 56 minutes,
4 seconds

Density: 5.5 (water = 1)

Known satellites:
1 moon

Surface area covered by ocean:
71 percent

Highest point above sea level:
Mount Everest,
5.5 miles
8.8 kilometers

Deepest part of ocean:
Challenger Deep, Marianas
Trench, Pacific Ocean,
6.9 miles
11 kilometers

Highest recorded temperature:
at Al 'Aziziyah, Libya,
136° F.
58° C.

Lowest recorded temperature:
at Vostok, Antarctica,
−126.9° F.
−88.3° C.

VIEW FROM SPACE: As seen from the Moon, Earth is a blue ball with swirls of white clouds all over the surface.

aurora

aurora

radio wave

thermosphere
beyond 51 mi/85 km

mesosphere
30–50 mi/50–80 km

stratosphere
7–30 mi/12–50 km

troposphere
0–7 mi/0–12 km

Aerospace

Y OU CANNOT FEEL THE weight because your body is used to the air pressing on it, but Earth's atmosphere is very heavy. In total it weighs about 5,000 trillion tons. The normal air pressure at sea level is 14.7 pounds per square inch (1.03 kilograms per square centimeter). Ordinarily you have about 10 tons of air pressing on your body.

Our atmosphere extends upward several hundred miles, but most of it is near the ground. The air becomes rapidly less dense as we go higher. Some people have trouble breathing the thin air on high mountains. When you go up 4 miles (6 kilometers), there is only half as much air as there is on the ground. When you fly in a jet airplane or in a spacecraft, you must take along the air you need to breathe. The air at sea level consists of about 78 percent nitrogen, 21 percent oxygen, and small amounts of water vapor, carbon dioxide, and other gases.

The atmosphere protects us from getting an overdose of sunshine during the day and keeps in enough heat so that we do not freeze at night. Most people spend their lives in the atmosphere's lowest layer, called the troposphere. In it are the oxygen that we breathe and all kinds of weather.

The troposphere extends upward to about 7 miles (12 kilometers). Above the troposphere is the stratosphere, which reaches an altitude of about 30 miles (50 kilometers).

Still higher is the ionosphere—from about 40 miles (70 kilometers). The ionosphere contains electrical particles that reflect radio waves to receiving stations far from broadcasting stations. An ozone layer blocks out deadly ultraviolet rays from the Sun. When electrical charges crash into the upper atmosphere, its gases glow colorfully. These lights are called auroras.

Earth's atmosphere is made up of many layers (left). They protect us from too much sunshine during the day and keep in needed heat at night.

The Moon

S O FAR, OUR MOON IS the only other world in space that humans have walked on. Six manned Apollo landings found the Moon to be a desolate place. It has no air, no water, and no living things.

The Moon's sky is always black because without air sunlight is not scattered. Astronauts on the Moon see both stars and a bright Sun in the daytime sky. Sound doesn't travel through empty space. In order for astronauts to talk to each other, they use two-way radios.

Because the Moon has no air or water, it has no weather—no clouds, no rain, no wind. Plants don't grow, nor do animals live. No microbes or fossil plants or animals have been found in any of the Moon rocks that the Apollo astronauts brought back to Earth. Although the Moon has no active volcanoes or strong moonquakes today, it had many several billion years ago. The Moon rocks are all igneous, which means that they were formed by the cooling of molten magma. The dark regions, called maria, are low, level areas that formed about 3 ½ billion years ago. The light parts, called highlands, are higher, more rugged, and older.

Unless people go and disturb it, the first human footprint on the Moon—made by Neil Armstrong—is expected to look the same for millions of years. The major source of change on the Moon is micrometeorites. These tiny grains of rock and metal crash into the surface at speeds of up to 70,000 miles (112,000 kilometers) per hour. They form craters and the lunar soil, a layer of powder and rubble 3 to 60 feet (1 to 20 meters) deep. Eons pass before the micrometeorites make an obvious difference.

In spite of the Moon's desolation, the Apollo astronauts showed that people can successfully live there when they bring their own air, water, and food from Earth. In the future, bases could be built on the Moon. Humans would wear spacesuits outside in order to maintain the same temperature and air pressure as on Earth.

An Apollo astronaut performs tests before he returns to his Moon rover. Earth shines in the sky.

MOON

The diameter of the Moon is .25 that of Earth.

Position from Sun: orbits Earth, third planet from the Sun

Average distance from Earth:
240,000 miles
384,400 kilometers

Diameter at equator:
2,170 miles
3,476 kilometers

Spins on axis in:
27.3 days

Phases repeat every:
29.5 days

Density: 3.34 (water = 1)

 A person who weighs 100 pounds on Earth would weigh 17 pounds on the Moon.

THROUGH A TELESCOPE: You can explore the Moon with binoculars or a small telescope. A full Moon is so bright that many interesting sights are lost in the glare. The best Moon observations can be made on clear evenings when the Moon is in its first quarter phase.

The map on pages 42–43 shows the side of the Moon you can see from Earth. Craters are named after famous scientists and philosophers such as Copernicus and Plato. Dark areas called maria (meaning "seas") were mistaken for oceans by their discoverer, Galileo Galilei (1564–1642). Actually dry lava beds, the maria have fanciful Latin names such as Mare Imbrium (Sea of Showers) and Mare Tranquillitatis (Sea of Tranquility). Mountain ranges are usually named after those on Earth, such as the Pyrenees and the Apennines.

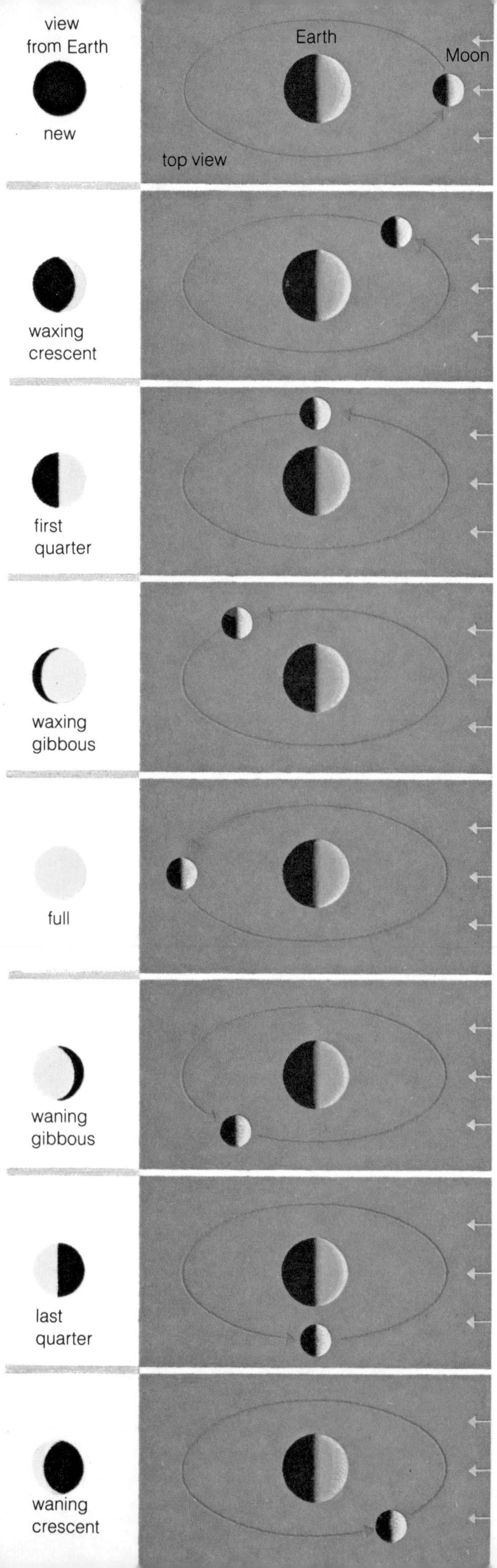

Phases, Tides, and Eclipses

view from Earth

new

waxing crescent

first quarter

waxing gibbous

full

waning gibbous

last quarter

waning crescent

Earth

Moon

top view

O UR MOON IS Earth's only natural satellite. It goes around our planet once every month, controlled by Earth's gravity. At the same time, Earth spins and travels around the Sun. All these motions affect the way the Moon appears in our sky. If you look at the Moon several times a week for a month, you will see interesting changes in its appearance.

Half the Moon is always lit by the Sun. As the Moon goes around Earth different amounts of its lighted part are visible to us. The various bright shapes we see from Earth are called the phases of the Moon.

A new Moon looks dark because its lighted side faces away from Earth. A few days later a thin crescent shines because a small part of the Moon's sunlit side faces Earth. After a week the right half of the first quarter Moon looks bright. After two weeks the full Moon's whole bright disk shines all night when the Moon has completed half of its monthly trip. The left half of the last quarter Moon looks bright after three weeks. After a total of 29½ days Earth, the Moon, and the Sun are lined up again. Then a new Moon shines once more and the phases repeat.

The Moon appears on the horizon about 50 minutes later each day than it did the day before. You can see the Moon rise in the east, cross the sky, and set in the west as Earth spins daily.

Daily ocean tides on Earth are caused mostly by the pull of the Moon's gravity. When the moon is overhead, its gravity pulls up the water below. The ocean under the Moon has high tide. The ocean on the opposite side of Earth also has high tide at the same time. Water flows from the other two sides of Earth to the high tide oceans. So those areas have low tides.

When the new Moon is directly between the Sun and Earth, an eclipse of the Sun occurs. If the Moon is relatively close to Earth, there is a total eclipse of the Sun. The total eclipse is visible from that part of Earth where the Moon's shadow falls. The Moon looks as big as the Sun because it is much closer. It blocks the Sun's bright disk from view. The sky gets darker and the air gets cooler. The Sun's corona is visible. Stars and planets

In the diagram at the left the arrows indicate the direction from which sunlight is streaming toward Earth. As the Moon travels around Earth each month, we can see different amounts of its sunlit part.

40

shine in the daytime. After a few minutes the Moon moves on. The Sun reappears and everything returns to normal.

If the Moon is relatively far from our planet, its shadow cone doesn't reach Earth and an annular eclipse occurs. Then the Moon blocks most of the Sun from view, leaving a bright ring of sunlight around its dark disk.

When the new Moon is not close enough to the Sun-Earth line to completely block the Sun's rays from anyplace on Earth, a partial eclipse occurs.

An eclipse of the Moon happens when the Sun, Earth, and full Moon are directly in line. The full Moon darkens when it moves into Earth's shadow. An eclipse of the Moon lasts over an hour. You can see it anyplace on Earth where the Moon is shining.

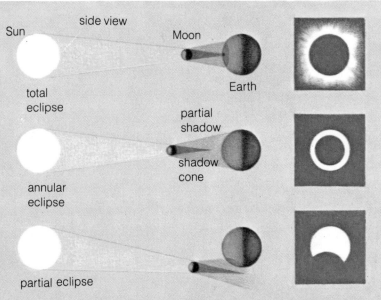

The kind of solar eclipse visible from Earth depends on how much sunlight the Moon blocks from view when it passes between the Sun and Earth.

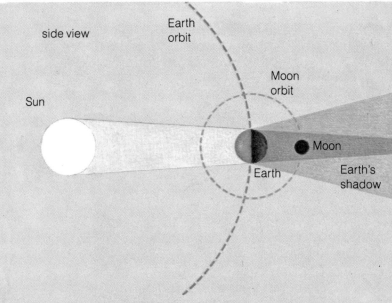

When the Moon moves into Earth's shadow, it is mostly hidden from view. This is called a lunar eclipse.

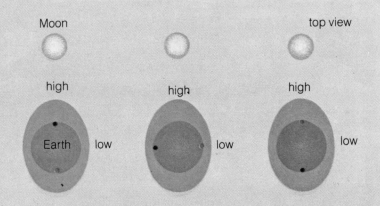

The area of ocean facing the Moon is pulled toward the Moon. There is a weaker pull on the water on Earth's opposite side. These are the areas of high tide. The two spots marked on each rotating Earth in the diagram show the same points at three different times during one day. The tide becomes high in the same area about every 12 hours and 25 minutes.

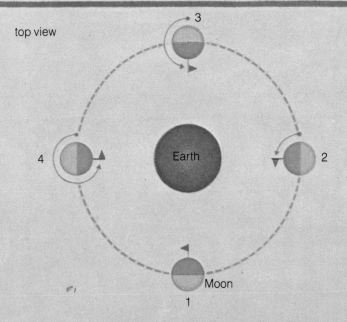

From Earth you can see just one side of the Moon. The Moon spins on its axis once in 27 1/3 days—the same amount of time it takes for the Moon to go around Earth once. So the same side of the Moon (blue in the diagram) always faces Earth.

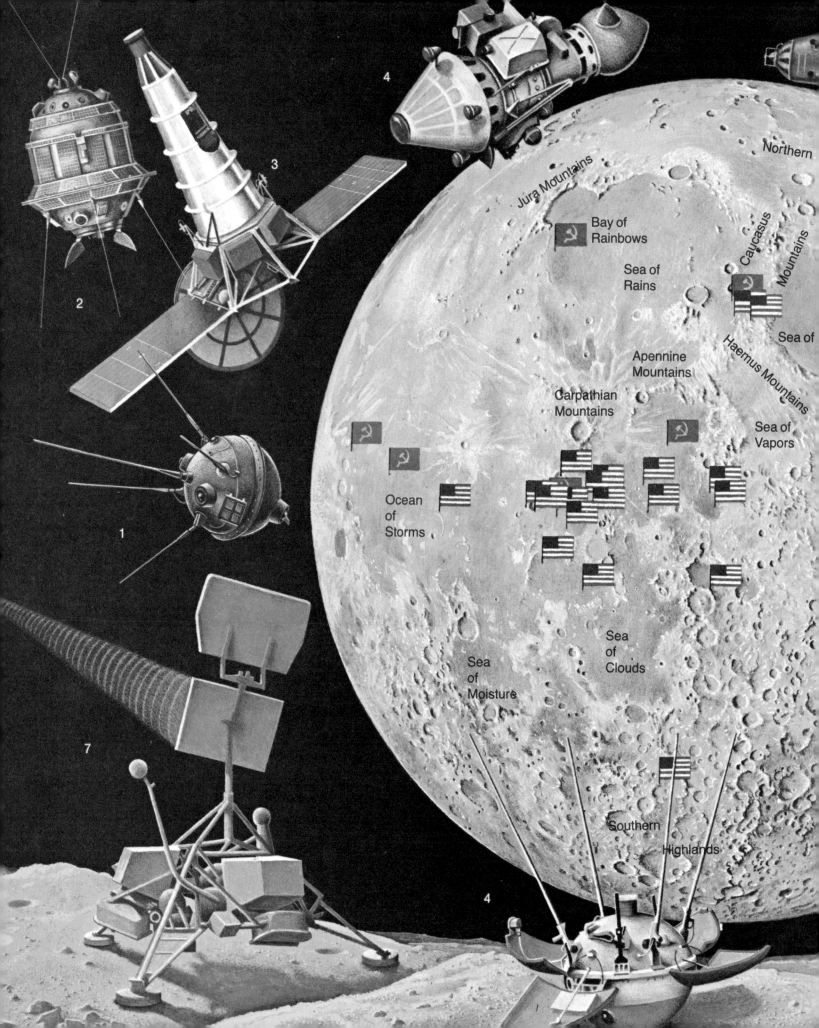

Jura Mountains

Northern

Bay of
Rainbows

Caucasus
Mountains

Sea of
Rains

Sea of

Haemus Mountains

Apennine
Mountains

Carpathian
Mountains

Sea of
Vapors

Ocean
of
Storms

Sea
of
Clouds

Sea
of
Moisture

Southern

Highlands

1

2

3

4

4

7

Highlands

Serenity

Sea of
Crises

Sea
of
Tranquility

Sea
of
Fertility

Sea
of
Nectar

Pyrenees
Mountains

5

6

8

9

10

Robot
Explorers

1. Luna 2 (USSR) was the first spacecraft to hit the Moon, on September 14, 1959.

2. On October 4, 1959, the Soviet Union launched Luna 3. As this spacecraft passed by the Moon it sent back the first photographs of the far side.

3. Ranger 7 (USA), launched on July 28, 1964, sent over 4,000 pictures before crashing into the Moon.

4. The first spacecraft to land on the Moon was the Luna 9 (USSR). The capsule soft-landed on February 3, 1966. It sent back pictures for three days.

5. On March 31, 1966, Luna 10 (USSR) was launched. It was the first craft to go into lunar orbit.

6. Between August 1966 and August 1967 the United States sent five lunar orbiter craft to the Moon. As these craft orbited they photographed the entire surface of the Moon. The photographs helped decide where the Apollo astronauts would land.

7. Surveyor spacecraft (USA) soft-landed on the Moon between May 1966 and January 1968. There were five successful missions that returned many photographs and also tested the lunar soil.

8. Explorer 35 (USA) entered orbit around the Moon on July 22, 1967, and measured Earth's magnetic fields.

9. The Soviet Union sent Luna 16 to the Moon on September 12, 1970. Luna 16 landed on September 20, scooped up several ounces of lunar soil, and returned to Earth on September 24.

10. Luna 17 (USSR) was launched on November 10, 1970, and landed on the Moon on November 17. It carried the Lunokhod 1, a self-propelled Moon roving vehicle.

The flags on the Moon pinpoint both robot (USA and USSR) and human (USA) explorations.

Apollo Mission Profile

ALL THE APOLLO spacecraft were launched from the Kennedy Space Center in Florida by the Saturn V rocket.

The first stage, with a thrust of 7.6 million pounds, boosted the spacecraft to a height of about 40 miles (65 kilometers), at a speed of about 6,000 miles (9,600 kilometers) per hour in about 2½ minutes (1). After engine shutdown the first stage separated and fell into the Atlantic Ocean. The second stage (2), with a thrust of 1 million pounds, carried the spacecraft to a height of about 115 miles (185 kilometers), at a speed of over 15,000 miles (25,000 kilometers) per hour. The second stage separated after engine cutoff and plunged into the Atlantic Ocean. The third stage (3) fired to put the craft in a circular orbit around Earth. After the crew performed a final systems check in Earth orbit, the third stage fired again to send the Apollo spacecraft toward the Moon.

The Apollo command/service module separated from the Saturn third stage (4). Then it turned around and docked with the lunar module, which was nested in the spacecraft lunar module adapter. Next the spacecraft was ejected from the third stage (5).

The Apollo command/service and lunar modules traveled together to the Moon (6).

After three days the spacecraft entered into orbit around the Moon, and two astronauts went into the lunar module. A third astronaut remained in the command module in orbit around the Moon (7). The lunar module separated and began its descent to the Moon's surface (8). As the lunar module neared the surface, rockets were fired to slow it down (9). The astronauts on board were able to take over from computer control and visually evaluate the landing site. After touchdown the landing crew got the lunar module ready for ascent, took a brief rest, and climbed out to explore the Moon (10). When their work was done, the astronauts climbed back into the ascent stage of the lunar module.

The ascent stage of the lunar module fired its rockets (11), taking the astronauts off the lunar surface and back into orbit around the Moon (12), where they docked with the command module (13). The landing crew took their Moon rocks and film into the command module. The lunar module ascent stage was jettisoned (14). The service module rocket was fired to send the craft back to Earth. Before reentry the service module was jettisoned (15). The command module, with the astronauts inside, returned to Earth.

The command module was encased in heat shields, which protected the astronauts as they traveled through Earth's atmosphere. Its blunt end faced forward (16). As the craft sped through the atmosphere, the temperature of the blunt heat shield rose to practically 5,000° F. (2,800° C.) (17). Three main parachutes were released to slow the spacecraft down to about 22 miles (35 kilometers) per hour (18). Splashdown occurred in the ocean. Recovery forces on waiting ships and aircraft picked up the astronauts and the Apollo command module.

Viking 1 approaches Mars.

Mars

MARS, THE RED PLANET, has fascinated people for thousands of years. Many were even convinced that strange civilizations flourished there. The fourth planet from the Sun, Mars gets enough sunshine to supply energy for living things, but robot explorers tell us that it is a cold, dry, apparently lifeless place.

With a diameter of 4,220 miles (6,790 kilometers), Mars is only half as big as Earth. It has as much land as Earth, since our planet has large oceans and Mars has none. Mars has neither lakes nor streams. No rain falls on Mars and there are large deserts on the planet. Wild dust storms which swirl out of the southern hemisphere in the summer can cover the whole planet.

Seasons on Mars resemble ours, but they last twice as long. Days on Mars are about the same as ours—24 hours each. The temperature drops as low as $-150°$ F.

$(-101°$ C.$)$ at night at the equator, colder than anywhere on Earth.

You could not breathe the air on Mars. It is 95 percent carbon dioxide gas. The air is almost one hundred times thinner than the air on Earth, and that is much too thin to keep you safe from the Sun's deadly ultraviolet rays. Your blood would boil on Mars.

Yet simple living things could survive on Mars. The air does have the basic ingredients living things need, including nitrogen, carbon, and oxygen. It has only one-thousandth as much water vapor as Earth's atmosphere. This small amount forms occasional fog and clouds.

Living things as we know them need water. Mars probably has frozen water underground. In some of the warmest places on the planet, pools of water may be trapped just below the surface. The north pole is capped by ice that is formed of frozen water. Ice on the south pole is mostly frozen water, with some frozen carbon dioxide (dry ice).

Mars looks like a bright red star in the sky. It orbits the Sun in 687 Earth days. Our view of the planet keeps changing because both Earth and Mars are moving. About every 780 days Mars looks brightest because then it is on the opposite side of Earth from the Sun and we can see its whole sunlit face. When Mars is behind the Sun, we cannot see it at all.

Mars is closest to Earth and looks brightest every 15 to 17 years because its orbit is elliptical. At its closest Mars is about 35 million miles (56 million kilometers) from Earth and looks like a small orange through a telescope. White icecaps spread over its north and south poles in the winter. In the summer they shrink in size. Irregular dark patterns sometimes cover part of the planet.

The Italian astronomer Giovanni Schiaparelli first reported seeing dark lines on Mars in 1877. He called them *canali*, which means ''channels'' in Italian, but it was mistranslated as ''canals.'' American astronomer Percival Lowell (1855–1916) later imagined incorrectly that intelligent Martians had built canals there.

Robot spacecraft have not taken any pictures of canals or Martians. The dark lines may actually be mountains. The irregular patterns could be dark rock uncovered by dust storms.

Two moons orbit Mars. They are small, cratered chunks of rock. Phobos, the inner moon, is about 13 miles (21 kilometers) long. It zips around the planet every seven and one-half hours. Phobos is covered with parallel grooves and with rows of small craters. One of its largest craters is named Hall—after the American astronomer Asaph Hall (1829–1907), who discovered the moons of Mars in 1877.

Deimos, the outer moon, is about 9 miles (15 kilometers) in diameter. It orbits Mars every thirty hours.

Earth revolves around the Sun more quickly than Mars does. At 1 and 2, Earth races to catch up with Mars. At 3, Earth passes Mars. Mars then appears to have moved backward from our perspective on Earth.

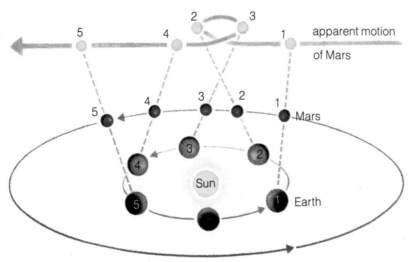

MARS

The diameter of Mars is .5 that of Earth.

Position from Sun: fourth planet

Average distance from Sun:
142,000,000 miles
228,000,000 kilometers

Diameter at equator:
4,220 miles
6,794 kilometers

Orbits Sun in:
687 days

Spins on axis in:
24 hours, 37 minutes

Density: 3.9 (water = 1)

 A person who weighs 100 pounds on Earth would weigh 38 pounds on Mars.

Known satellites:
2 moons: Phobos and Deimos

IN THE SKY: Mars looks like a bright red star. It orbits the Sun in 687 days outside Earth's path. Because we are moving and Mars is too, our view of the planet keeps changing. About every 780 days Mars looks brightest because it is on the opposite side of Earth from the Sun. We see its whole sunlit face. When Mars is behind the Sun, we can't see it at all.

THROUGH A TELESCOPE: When Mars is closest, it resembles a small orange. White icecaps spread over its north and south poles in the winter and shrink during the summer. Irregular dark patterns sometimes cover part of the planet.

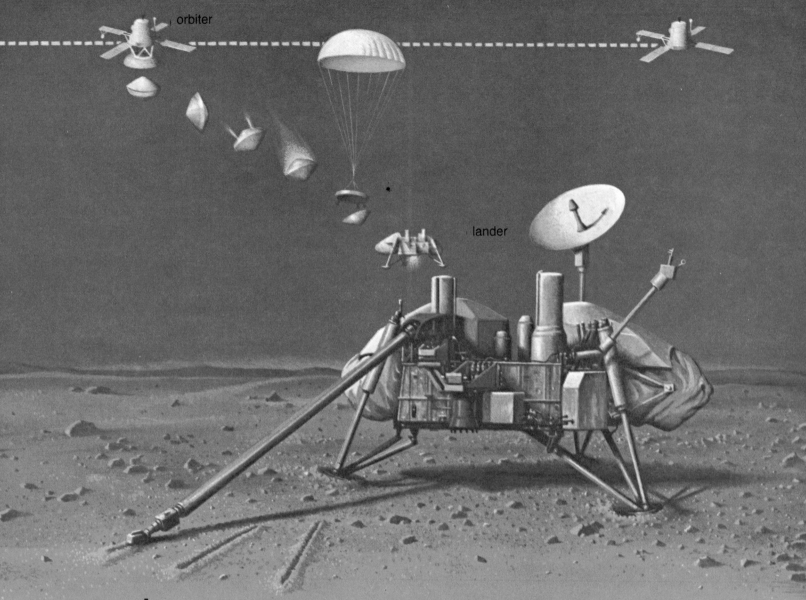

orbiter

lander

Exploring Mars

MORE ROBOT SPACECRAFT have explored Mars than any of our other neighboring planets. Mariner 4 in 1965 and Mariners 6 and 7 in 1969 flew by and transmitted pictures and information back to Earth. In 1971 Mariner 9 was the first spacecraft to orbit Mars. It successfully photographed the entire planet. Scientists used the photographs to make accurate planetary maps for the next visitors.

Viking 1 and Viking 2 arrived at Mars in 1976 to study its air and surface and to search for evidence of life. Each spacecraft consisted of two robot explorers. A lander gathered data and took pictures on the

ground. An orbiter worked hundreds of miles above the planet.

Each lander stands on three legs. It cannot walk. Two cameras are positioned like eyes standing 4 feet (1.3 meters) above the surface of the planet.

Each lander has one long arm with a claw at the end to scoop up soil for tests. Inside the lander are two power stations that give the robot its energy. Two computers serve as "brains." A weather station, two chemistry and three biology laboratories, and a seismometer (to measure ground movements) are packed into the lander's automobile-sized body. The information gathered is transmitted back to Earth for analysis.

Tests were done to detect indications of life processes, but the tests did not settle the question of the existence of living organisms on Mars.

Viking 1 found rocks of different sizes. Fine red dust covers darker rock, and sand piles up in dunes. The sky is colored pink in the daytime by sunlight bouncing off red dust in the air. The Red Planet gets its color from rusted iron in the soil.

The Vikings sent back thousands of pictures of the ground. A very thin layer of frost covers the rocks in winter. Craters indicate that Mars was bombarded by meteorites millions of years ago.

The next explorers on Mars will likely be sophisticated robots. They do not need air, water, food, or shelter, as people do. They could travel long distances over the surface of the planet and relay much information back to Earth.

People could live on Mars in a domed base or an underground colony with an environment much like Earth's. Outside the habitat they could wear spacesuits to protect themselves from the planet's deadly conditions.

There are gigantic volcanoes on Mars (right). The largest is Olympus Mons, or Mount Olympus. The top of this volcano pierces the clouds at a height of 15 miles (24 kilometers) above the surface. Olympus Mons is more than twice as tall as Mauna Kea in Hawaii, which is the tallest volcano on Earth. The enormous caldera, or crater, is 50 miles (80 kilometers) wide. The whole state of Rhode Island could easily fit inside this huge crater.

There are also huge canyons on Mars (left). They were probably produced by a tremendous cracking of the crust of the planet billions of years ago. The largest canyon is called Valles Marineris, or Mariner Valley. It is 3,000 miles (5,000 kilometers) long. If it were on Earth, it would stretch from New York City to San Francisco. At some points the enormous canyon is 3 miles (5 kilometers) deep and 150 miles (240 kilometers) wide. Our own Earth's great Grand Canyon would be lost inside Valles Marineris.

There are channels on Mars that look as though they had been carved by great rivers (right). These channels are deep and winding. The Viking space probes detected water ice and vapor on the planet, but no flowing water. A long time ago, however, Mars may have been warmer, and perhaps at that time it had great streams. That water may now be frozen at the poles and underground. If it is true that Mars was once warmer and had flowing water, simple living things could have developed there. If they did, they could still be in the soil or in the rocks today.

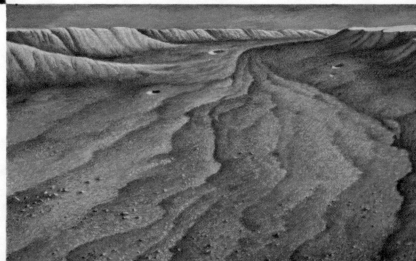

Jupiter

THE PLANET JUPITER is bigger and heavier than all of the other planets and their moons combined. It is larger in volume than 1,300 Earths put together.

If Jupiter were eighty times more massive, this giant would be hot enough to shine as a star. Still, it gives off about twice as much heat as it receives from the Sun. The planet also emits radio signals and X rays.

Jupiter looks very different from our planet Earth. We can see only its colorful and constantly moving thick clouds. Beneath this heavy cloud cover Jupiter is apparently a gigantic spinning liquid ball without a firm surface. It may have a core that is rocky and made of iron and about the same size as Earth's.

Jupiter is made mostly of hydrogen, with some helium. In its clouds are traces of colorless methane, ammonia, water vapor, and other gases. Still other chemicals must give the clouds their brilliant color.

The cloud tops of Jupiter are very cold. Temperatures there can run as low as $-200°$ F. $(-130°$ C.). Lightning flashes in the thick atmosphere, and auroras appear near the poles. Most likely the hydrogen gets denser and warmer farther down through the clouds. In the core the temperature could be 53,000° F. (30,000° C.) or higher.

Jupiter's magnetic field is much more powerful than Earth's, and its strength changes. Sometimes its force can be felt 9 million miles (14.5 million kilometers) sunward and nearly 500 million miles (800 million kilometers) outward—even beyond Saturn's orbit.

The Great Red Spot of Jupiter is a tremendous storm in the atmosphere. Every six days it travels completely around the planet. Observers have been watching the Great Red Spot for more than 300 years. Much bigger than Earth, the Great Red Spot is about 9,000 miles (14,000 kilometers) wide, and up to 25,000 miles (40,000 kilometers) long. Its size, brightness, and color change. Clouds in the Great Red Spot swirl high above their neighbors in a counterclockwise direction.

Countless tiny particles and large rocks whiz around Jupiter. Reflecting sunlight, they ring the planet. The ring extends some 34,000 miles (57,000 kilometers) outward from Jupiter's cloud tops.

Jupiter shines more brightly than any other planet except Venus. It reflects a great deal of sunlight because it is the biggest of the planets and is completely wrapped in clouds.

With a telescope you can see the Great Red Spot, stripes of clouds, and Jupiter's four largest moons—Io, Europa, Ganymede, and Callisto. The moons look like tiny bright dots. Because they orbit the planet, they are in a different position every night.

Four American spacecraft have flown by Jupiter. In 1973 and 1974 Pioneer 10 and Pioneer 11 sent the first close-up photographs back to Earth. In 1979 Voyager 1 and Voyager 2 (left) returned important data and more than 33,000 spectacular photographs.

JUPITER

The diameter of Jupiter is 11.2 times greater than that of Earth.

Position from Sun: fifth planet

Average distance from Sun:
484,000,000 miles
778,400,000 kilometers

Diameter at equator:
89,000 miles
143,200 kilometers

Orbits Sun in:
11.9 years

Spins on axis in:
9 hours, 56 minutes

Density: 1.3 (water = 1)

 A person who weighs 100 pounds on Earth would weigh 234 pounds on Jupiter.

Known satellites:
16 moons
Rings

IN THE SKY: Jupiter shines more brightly than any other planet except Venus. The planet reflects a lot of sunlight because it is the biggest planet and is completely wrapped in clouds.

THROUGH A TELESCOPE: You can see the Great Red Spot, stripes of clouds, and Jupiter's four largest moons—Io, Europa, Ganymede, and Callisto. The moons look like tiny bright dots. You can see that they orbit the planet because they're in a different position every night.

Jupiter's Moons

THERE ARE SIXTEEN KNOWN moons orbiting Jupiter. Io, Europa, Ganymede, and Callisto are the largest and shine the brightest. They are called the Galilean moons in honor of the Italian astronomer Galileo Galilei (1564–1642), who discovered them. The other moons are small and still mostly unknown.

Io and Europa are about the size of our Moon, but they look very different. Neither has many impact craters. Europa shines brightest because of its smooth, icy surface. Io is brilliantly colored and is the only moon known to have active volcanoes.

Both Ganymede and Callisto are bigger than Mercury. Ganymede is the largest known moon in the solar system. Callisto looks ancient. It has many craters that look like they have not changed in 4 billion years. Both seem to be made half of water and half of rocky material.

A gigantic cloud wobbles around Jupiter at the distance of Io. It is made of electrically charged bits of sulfur and oxygen, probably hurled outward from Io's volcanoes.

Io's brilliant colors come from chemical compounds of sulfur brought to the surface by violent volcanic eruptions. Volcanoes are in the dark spots. Frosty plains between the volcanoes have few features. Io's surface appears to be only about 10 million years old, quite young for a moon.

Europa is covered with streaks that look as though they are breaks in the thin ice crust. Below the ice there is most likely a warmer layer of slush, about 60 miles (100 kilometers) thick, and a rocky core. Fresh ice or snow along the cracks and cold glacier-like flows could have erased impact craters.

Ganymede has dark areas with many craters like the Moon. These dark areas are more than 4 billion years old. Younger, lighter areas, with grooves and faults, suggest that Ganymede was geologically active more than 3 billion years ago.

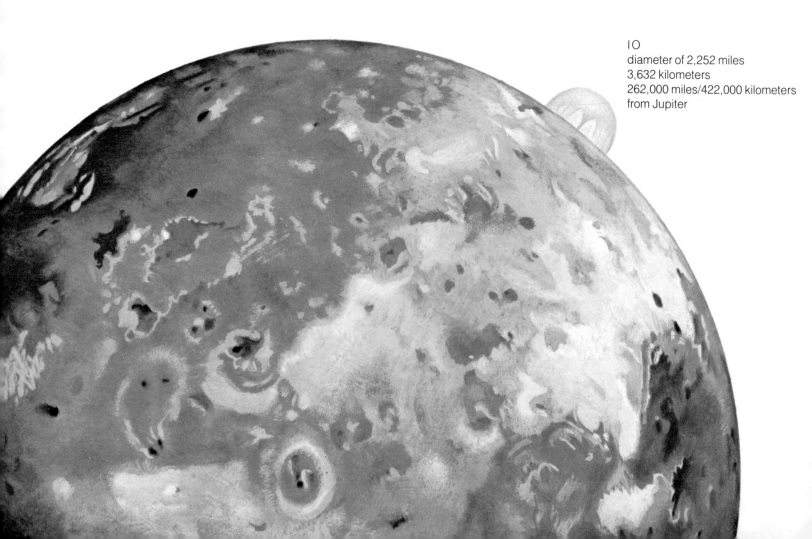

IO
diameter of 2,252 miles
3,632 kilometers
262,000 miles/422,000 kilometers
from Jupiter

Callisto is covered with impact craters. It looks like our Moon and the planet Mercury. Apparently Callisto's surface has changed little since many meteorites bombarded it more than 4 billion years ago.

Voyager 1 took the first close look ever at small Amalthea. About the size of California, this moon looks dark red and has many craters.

CALLISTO
diameter of 2,988 miles
4,820 kilometers
1,166,000 miles/1,880,000 kilometers
from Jupiter

GANYMEDE
diameter of 3,271 miles
5,276 kilometers
663,000 miles/1,070,000 kilometers
from Jupiter
Ganymede is the largest known moon in the solar system.

EUROPA
diameter of 1,938 miles
3,126 kilometers
418,000 miles/671,000 kilometers
from Jupiter

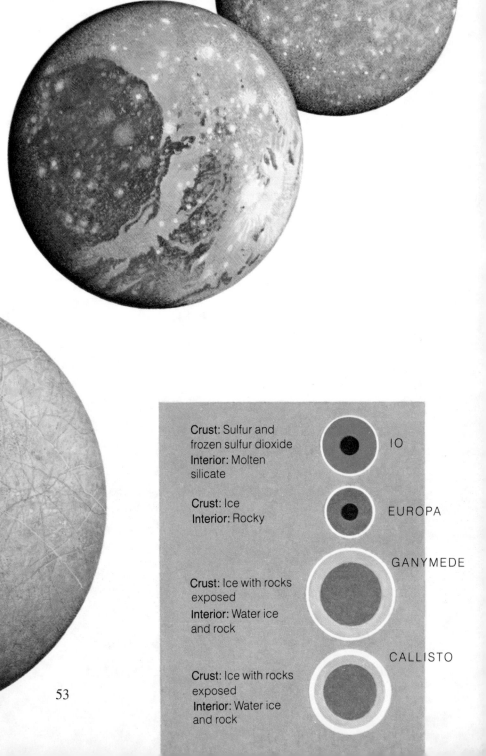

Crust: Sulfur and frozen sulfur dioxide
Interior: Molten silicate
IO

Crust: Ice
Interior: Rocky
EUROPA

Crust: Ice with rocks exposed
Interior: Water ice and rock
GANYMEDE

Crust: Ice with rocks exposed
Interior: Water ice and rock
CALLISTO

53

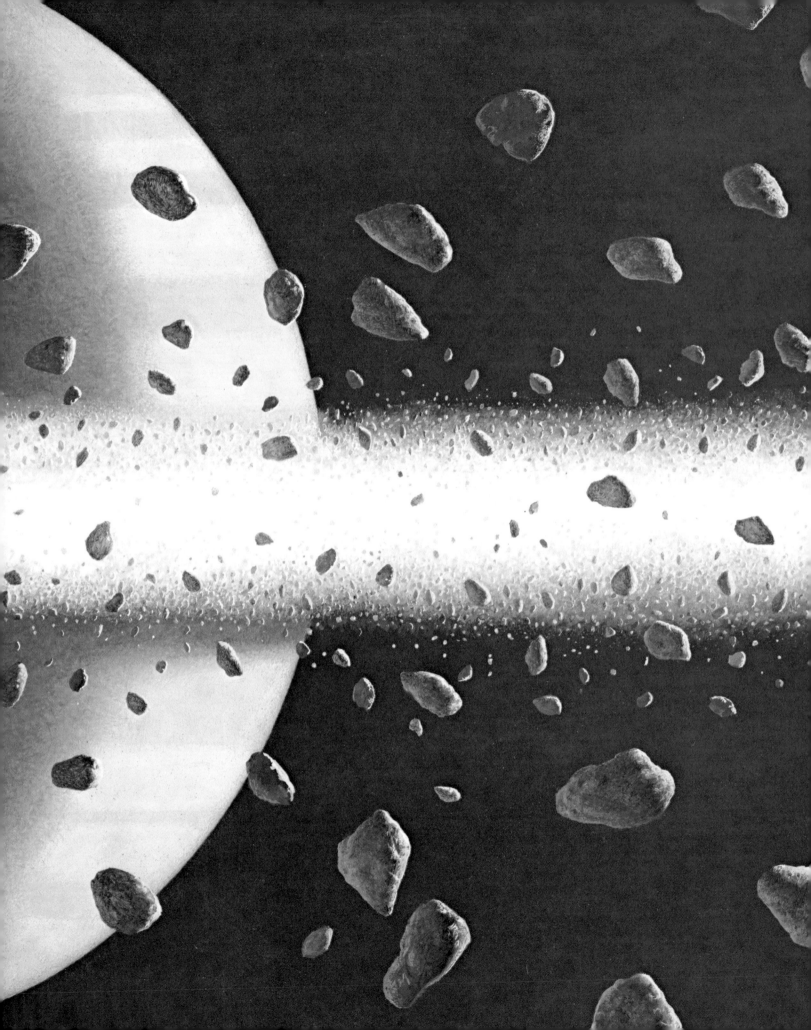

Saturn

THE DAZZLING RINGS around Saturn have fascinated observers for centuries. When Galileo first saw them in his small telescope, he said they resembled ears attached to Saturn. Using a better telescope, the Dutch astronomer Christian Huygens (1629–1695) correctly described the true form of the rings in 1655.

The rings consist of countless particles of ice or ice-covered rock, orbiting Saturn. They range in size from microscopic to several yards across. The icy particles shine by reflecting sunlight. In small telescopes the rings look solid because they are so far from Earth.

Saturn, the second largest planet in our solar system, could hold 758 Earths inside it. The planet weighs more than 95 times as much as Earth. However, it is so big that it has the lowest density of all the planets. If there were a gigantic ocean to put it in, Saturn would not sink.

Saturn resembles Jupiter in many ways. It is a huge spinning gas ball consisting mainly of hydrogen with some helium, and it may have a rocky core. Because it spins so fast, it is flattened at its poles. It sends out radio signals.

Thick and constantly moving clouds completely envelop the planet. The belts and zones do not look as colorful or as clear as Jupiter's because they are under a thicker haze. Ovals resembling Jupiter's large storm areas are visible, but the details inside are not.

Strong, high-speed winds blow, especially at the equator. The cloud tops are cold—below −300° F. (−190° C.). Auroras occur near the poles.

Saturn acts as a powerful magnet, although not as strong as Jupiter. At times its magnetic force can be felt more than 1 million miles (2 million kilometers) away on the Sun side. The magnetic field drags along electrically charged bits that travel around Saturn.

From Voyager 1's view, an edge-on look at the swirling ice, rock, and dust that make up Saturn's rings. The rings stretch over 40,000 miles (65,000 kilometers) but are only a few miles thick.

Saturn's Moons

THE MOST INTERESTING of Saturn's moons is Titan. The second largest known moon in the solar system, Titan measures about 3,200 miles (5,150 kilometers) across. Titan is the only moon known to have a substantial atmosphere. The atmosphere is mostly nitrogen, with hydrocarbons such as methane and ethane, which color it orange. The atmosphere is the source of an enormous cloud of hydrogen that rings Saturn between the orbits of Titan and Rhea. Beneath the haze Titan apparently has a surface made of rock and ice. There may be liquid pools. Certainly this moon, which orbits 758,600 miles (1,221,860 kilometers) from Saturn, has exciting possibilities for future discoveries.

Phoebe is the most distant of Saturn's moons at 8,049,000 miles (12,954,000 kilometers). It is very dark, roughly spherical, and about 137 miles (220 kilometers) across. It rotates approximately once every 9 hours. Since Phoebe orbits Saturn in a retrograde (backward) direction in an unusual plane, it may be a captured asteroid that formed somewhere else in the solar system.

Closer to Saturn, at 2,208,000 miles (3,561,000 kilometers), is Iapetus. Iapetus has the widest known range of albedo values (the fraction of sunlight reflected back to space) of any body in the solar system. The leading face of Iapetus in its orbital motion is covered with dark material, which could have come from space. The trailing face has craters with dark floors that may have originated from activity inside the moon.

Hyperion has an irregular shape about 260 miles (410 kilometers) by 160 miles (260 kilometers) wide. Its rather dark surface still has many craters from heavy bombardment by meteorites. They suggest that Hyperion's surface is very old and that there is no activity inside the moon to change it.

Rhea is about 950 miles (1,530 kilometers) across. Most of its surface is covered with craters, craters, and more craters. Three parts of Rhea's surface show large circular plains with fewer craters. Perhaps these are the results of large rocks that crashed into Rhea's surface and formed great craters, which filled up with slush and then froze. Rhea is about 327,500 miles (527,100 kilometers) from Saturn.

Dione looks similar to Rhea. Its icy surface is covered with craters and a system of valleys. It is about 696 miles (1,120 kilometers) wide and 234,500 miles (377,420 kilometers) from Saturn. The largest feature is a white spot named Amata. Amata may be a large crater filled in with fairly new ice. Most of the craters seem to have flat floors, which suggests that the impact that formed them caused the icy surface to melt, flow into the bottom of the crater, and then refreeze.

Tethys is about 183,000 miles (294,700 kilometers) from Saturn. This moon is 650 miles (1,050 kilometers) wide and has an enormous impact crater that is almost 250 miles (400 kilometers) wide. The crater, with its large peak at the center, may have formed long ago when Tethys was relatively warm. A great fracture, called Ithaca Chasma, goes almost three quarters of the way around the moon. Astronomers believe that

To date 22 moons of Saturn are known. The larger moons are labeled in the illustration below. Further study of data may reveal more moons.

Titan is covered by a thick atmosphere.

Tethys is almost pure ice and that as the moon froze, it cracked, forming this huge valley.

About 147,900 miles (238,040 kilometers) from the planet, Enceladus is over 300 miles (500 kilometers) wide. It has the most active surface of any of Saturn's moons. The youngest part looks less than a few million years old. The surface is probably still changing. Perhaps the changes are due to heating that occurs because Dione tugs on Enceladus as the two moons orbit Saturn. The resulting friction and heat could melt the icy surface, which could then flow into craters and refreeze. The end result is the constant resurfacing of the moon.

Mimas orbits 115,300 miles (185,540 kilometers) from Saturn. It is 246 miles (396 kilometers) wide and has a surprisingly large crater several miles wide. Mimas' craters have flat floors, which suggests that the impacts that formed the craters caused surface melting of material and later refroze.

The diameter of Saturn is 9.4 times greater than that of Earth.

Position from Sun: sixth planet

Average distance from Sun:
885,000,000 miles
1,425,600,000 kilometers

Diameter at equator:
75,000 miles
120,000 kilometers

Orbits Sun in:
29.5 years

Spins on axis in:
10 hours, 40 minutes

Density: 0.7 (water = 1)

A person who weighs 100 pounds on Earth would weigh 93 pounds on Saturn.

Known satellites:
22 sighted moons
Rings

IN THE SKY: Thousands of years ago people thought Saturn was the planet farthest from the Sun. It is the most distant planet you can readily spot without a telescope.

THROUGH A TELESCOPE: You can see Saturn's dazzling rings and its largest moon, Titan. Year after year the rings look different. They always point the same way in space as Saturn goes around the Sun. They just seem to change their tilt because we observe them from different spots along Earth's orbit.

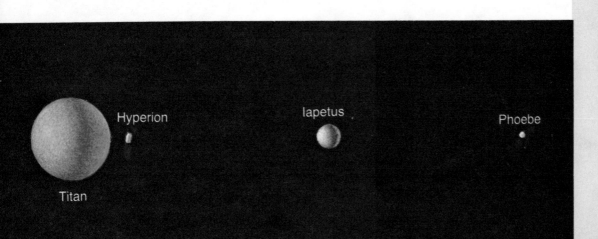

Titan   Hyperion   Iapetus   Phoebe

Uranus

U NTIL 1781 ONLY five planets were known. That year the German musician-astronomer Sir William Herschel (1738-1822) first noted Uranus. He mistook its small, round shape for a comet. People began to study the object, and several months later they had determined that it was a planet—the first to be discovered with a telescope.

From Earth we can see only the cloud tops of Uranus. The deep, cold, clear atmosphere is mostly hydrogen and some helium. The blue-green color results from the absorption of red light by methane gas. Scientists think that Uranus has a central core of rock and metal surrounded by layers of ice, liquid hydrogen, and hydrogen gas.

Fifteen known moons orbit Uranus. Miranda, Ariel, Umbriel, Titania, and Oberon are the largest. Voyager 2 sent back the first close-ups of them in 1986. Their dark gray surfaces have craters, fault systems, canyons, and volcanic material. They seem to be made of ice and rock. Oberon and Titania are about half the size of Earth's moon, some 1,000 miles (1,600 kilometers) across. Narrow rings of particles, from tiny dust grains to chunks as big as boulders, also circle the planet. They were discovered in 1977 from NASA's Kuiper Airborne Observatory. The observatory is an airplane that flies a telescope, other instruments, and scientists above most of Earth's atmosphere. Uranus is just bright enough to be seen when stargazing conditions are best. Uranus looks faint because it is 2 billion miles (3 billion kilometers) away from the Sun, its source of light. With the unaided eye, it looks like a very faint star. Through a telescope the distant planet looks like a small bright disk, without clear features.

The diameter of Uranus is 4 times greater than that of Earth.

Position from Sun: seventh planet

Average distance from Sun:
1,780,000,000 miles
2,867,000,000 kilometers

Diameter at equator:
32,200 miles
51,800 kilometers

Orbits Sun in:
84 years

Spins on axis in:
About 16 hours

Density: 1.2 (water = 1)

A person who weighs 100 pounds on Earth would weigh 85 pounds on Uranus.

Known satellites:
15 moons
Rings

IN THE SKY: Uranus is just bright enough to be seen when stargazing conditions are best. It looks like a very faint star. The ancients may have seen Uranus but didn't call it a planet.

Uranus looks very faint to us because it is so far away both from the Sun, which lights it, and from Earth. It is almost 2 billion miles (3 billion kilometers) away.

THROUGH A TELESCOPE: You can see a small bright disk. Features are not clear to us because Uranus is so far from Earth.

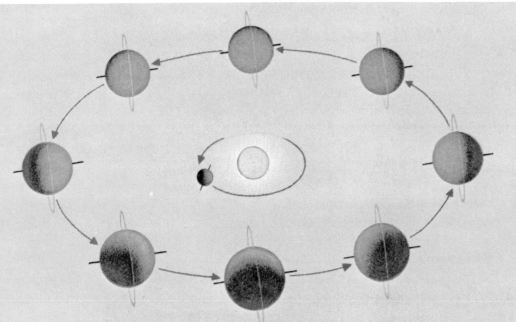

The axis of Uranus is exceptional. It is practically in the plane of the planet's orbit. Where the other planets have their equators, Uranus has its poles. As Uranus revolves around the sun (above) once every 84 years, its axis always points in the same direction. For 42 years one pole is in sunlight and the other pole is in darkness. During the next 42 years these conditions are reversed. Five moons orbit Uranus (left), and narrow rings encircle the planet.

NEPTUNE

The diameter of Neptune is almost 4 times greater than that of Earth.

Position from Sun: eighth planet

Average distance from Sun:
2,790,000,000 miles
4,486,000,000 kilometers

Diameter at equator:
30,800 miles
49,500 kilometers

Orbits Sun in:
164 years

Spins on axis in:
About 17 hours, 50 minutes

Density: 1.7 (water = 1)

 A person who weighs 100 pounds on Earth would weigh 114 pounds on Neptune.

Known satellites:
2 moons: Triton and Nereid

IN THE SKY: You can't spot Neptune without binoculars or a telescope. It is too faint to see because it is so far away both from the Sun, which lights it, and from Earth. It is almost 3 billion miles (4.5 billion kilometers) away.

THROUGH A TELESCOPE: You can see a small disk. Features are not clear even in big telescopes because Neptune is so far away from us.

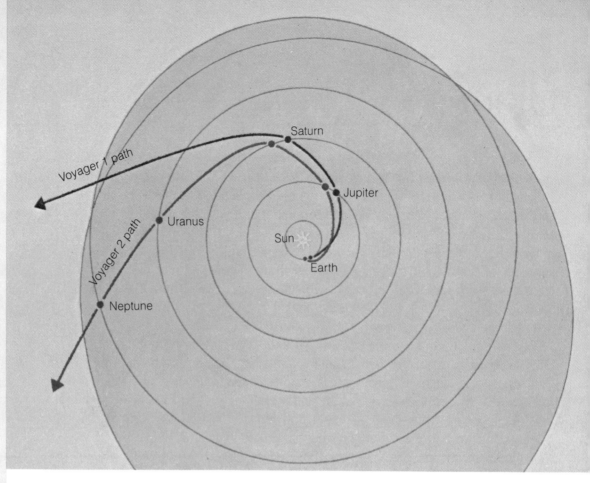

Voyager 1 and Voyager 2 left Earth in the summer of 1977. Voyager 2 flew by Saturn in August 1981 and used the planet's gravity to put it on a path so that it would intercept the orbits of Uranus in 1986 and Neptune in 1989.

Neptune

AFTER URANUS WAS discovered, scientists observed that it did not orbit exactly as they had expected. John Adams in England and Urbain Leverrier in France each did some mathematical calculations. They figured that another, more distant planet was tugging on Uranus. In 1846 Johann Galle pointed his telescope toward the spot where they predicted the new planet would be and found the planet Neptune.

You can't see Neptune with your unaided eye. Through binoculars or a telescope it looks like a small, bright disk. Its features are not clear even in big telescopes, since it is almost 3 billion miles (4.5 billion kilometers) from Earth.

From Earth we see only the top of Neptune's very deep atmosphere. So far hydrogen and methane have been detected there, and there is probably helium too. Scientists think Neptune has a structure like that of Uranus. Under its thin outer atmosphere are thicker layers of gases and then liquids, mostly hydrogen. Inside is a layer of ice and then a core made of rock and iron.

Neptune has two known moons and probably rings. Triton, bigger and heavier than our Moon, circles Neptune in six of our days. Triton looks as if it is very close to Neptune and seems to be in danger of being torn apart by Neptune's gravity. Nereid, smaller and much farther from Neptune, takes about a year to circle the planet.

Voyager 2 will reach Neptune after twelve years of travel through space. In 1989 it could give us our first look at Neptune.

Pluto

The diameter of Pluto is about .25 that of Earth.

THE SEARCH FOR a ninth planet began when Uranus and Neptune did not travel as scientists calculated they should. American astronomer Percival Lowell predicted that they were being tugged by another planet's gravity. Clyde Tombaugh was assigned the job of looking for this planet at the Lowell Observatory in Flagstaff, Arizona. After studying many thousands of pictures of small parts of the sky, Tombaugh discovered Pluto in 1930.

Pluto travels farther from the Sun and Earth than any other planet we know. If you were standing on Pluto, you would see the Sun as a bright star in the sky. You would get only 1/1600 the amount of sunshine you get on Earth. Pluto is bitter cold. Its orbit is tilted and stretched out so that sometimes it travels inside Neptune's orbit. Pluto is now closer than Neptune to the Sun. Pluto will get closest to the Sun in 1989. Not until 1999 will it move beyond Neptune again.

Some scientists think Pluto is a moon that escaped from Neptune. Others think it was wandering through space when the Sun's gravity captured it. Still others believe it formed with the other planets almost 5 billion years ago. Pluto is too far away to be seen with your unaided eye or even with binoculars or a small telescope. Even large telescopes picture Pluto only as a small, bright disk without any features. Pluto appears to be like a big orbiting snowball. Outside it is covered by methane ice that reflects sunshine brightly. Inside it may have rocks and frozen methane and water. Pluto is apparently not heavy enough for its gravity to pull Uranus and Neptune out of their regular paths. So there is a chance that our Sun has a yet undiscovered tenth planet that tugs on them.

Pioneer 10 left Earth in 1972 bound for Jupiter. In 1983 it was the first spacecraft to leave the outer limits of our solar system. It did not fly close enough to Pluto to tell us anything about this distant world.

Position from Sun: ninth planet

Average distance from Sun:
3,660,000,000 miles
5,890,000,000 kilometers

Diameter at equator:
930 miles (?)
1,500 kilometers (?)

Orbits Sun in:
247 years

Spins on axis in:
6 days, 9 hours (?)

Density: 0.5 (?) (water = 1)

 A person who weighs 100 pounds on Earth would weigh 4.5 pounds (?) on Pluto.

Known satellites:
1 moon: Charon

IN THE SKY: You can never see Pluto shining in our sky because it is too small and too far away.

THROUGH A TELESCOPE: You need a large telescope to spot Pluto. The world's biggest telescopes picture a small bright disk without any features. Pluto remains a mysterious place. Even its size is not definitely known yet.

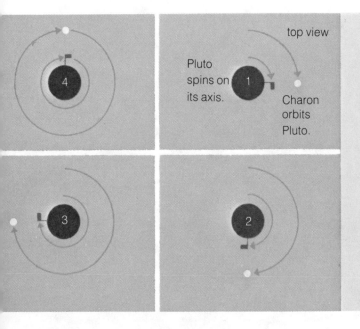

top view

Pluto spins on its axis.

Charon orbits Pluto.

In 1978 American astronomer James W. Christy noticed a bump on Pluto in his pictures. This turned out to be a moon orbiting Pluto. Ten thousand miles (17,000 kilometers) above Pluto, Charon circles the planet in 6 days, 9 hours. Pluto makes one complete rotation in exactly the same time. As you can see from the diagram on the left, if you were on the same side of Pluto as Charon, you would always see Charon at the same place in the sky. If you were on the opposite side of Pluto, you would never even get a glimpse of Charon.

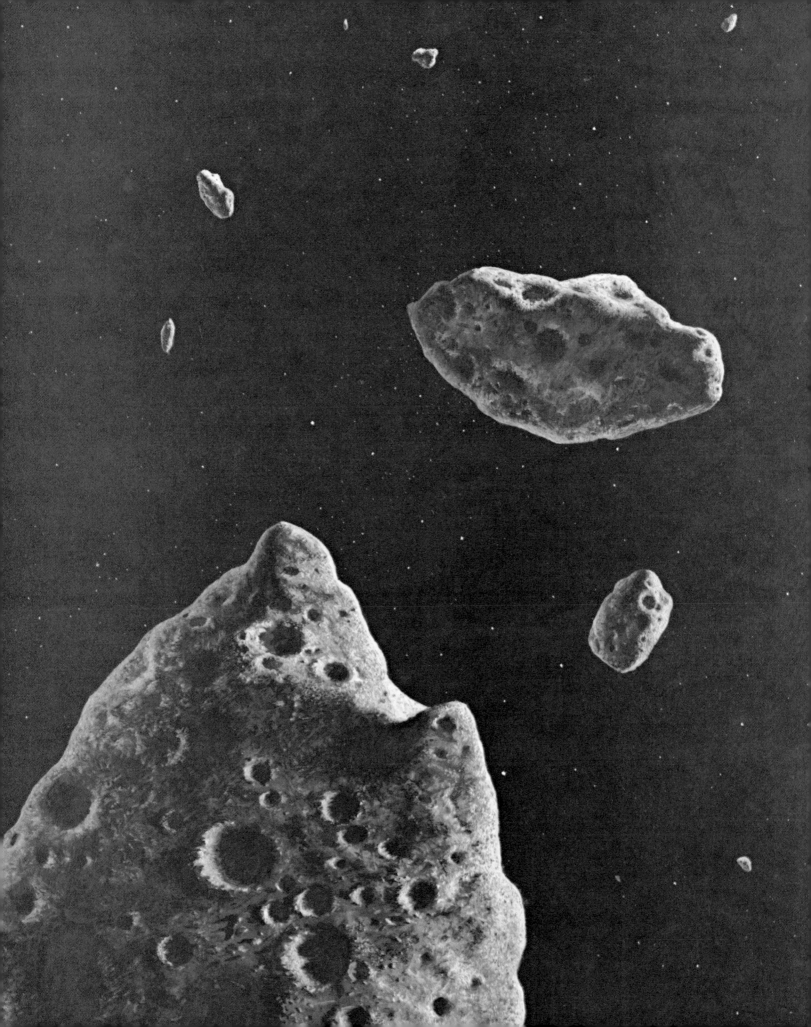

Asteroids

THOUSANDS OF ROCKS CALLED asteroids, or minor planets, orbit the Sun. The biggest is Ceres, which is almost as wide as Texas. More than 3,000 smaller asteroids of different sizes have been discovered in the space between Mars and Jupiter. Millions more tinier ones probably exist there. Together all of these asteroids probably weigh less than our Moon. In 1977 an object named Chiron, which may be an asteroid, was discovered between Saturn and Uranus. It is the first found in an outer zone.

The big asteroids most likely formed at the same time as the Sun—about 5 billion years ago. They are clumps of material that never grew big enough to form a planet. Some of the asteroids contain carbon compounds and water. These same chemicals are necessary for all the plants and animals on Earth. Apparently the raw materials for living things have been in space ever since our solar system began.

A group of more than 25 asteroids called Apollo objects come close enough to Earth for possible visits in the future. A robot spacecraft could photograph them first. By the 1990s robot spacecraft could make round-trip flights to the larger asteroids. They could land and collect and bring back samples for study in the laboratory. Asteroids could be a rich source of metals and water for future space colonists.

In the twenty-first century some asteroids might be towed into orbits around Earth and their resources used by space colonists or transported back to Earth to be used here.

Asteroids look like stars through a telescope. The word "asteroid" means "like a star."

ASTEROID ORBITS

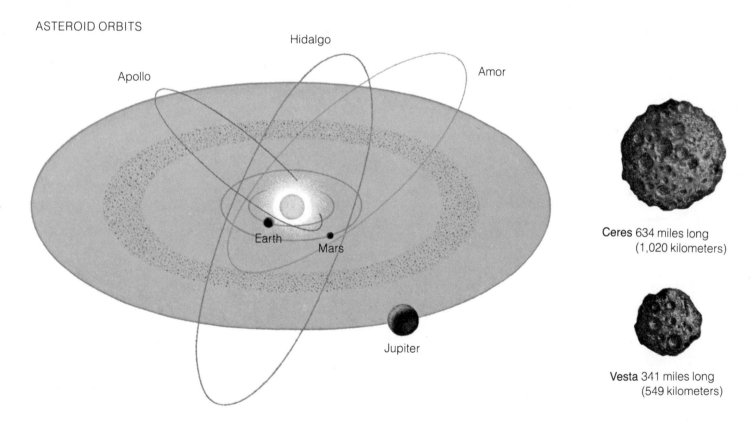

Ceres 634 miles long (1,020 kilometers)

Vesta 341 miles long (549 kilometers)

The Apollo asteroids cross Earth's orbit and sometimes penetrate it. Eros, the largest Apollo asteroid, is 10 miles (16 kilometers) long, practically the size of New York City. Eros last came close to Earth at 15.5 million miles (22.5 million kilometers) in January 1975.

Most Apollo asteroids are less than a mile wide. If one crashed into Earth, it could destroy our biggest cities. But there is no need to worry—the chances of such a crash are extremely small.

Comets

Long ago people thought that comets were signs of bad luck. They were terrified when a comet appeared in the sky; bright comets were considered omens of war, famine, disease, and other disasters.

Today we recognize comets as members of our solar system. They travel along orbits, controlled by the Sun's gravity. But comets are still puzzling, and no one can predict when a new one will appear.

Billions of comets probably orbit the Sun beyond Pluto. Occasionally a passing star may tug on a comet and send it plunging toward the Sun. If it passes near Jupiter, that planet's strong gravity may put it into a new orbit.

American astronomer Fred Whipple likened a comet to a dirty snowball. When a comet is far from the Sun, it is a frozen ball of gases, such as carbon dioxide, ammonia, methane, and water vapor (the ''snow''), and stony or metallic particles (the ''dirt''). A comet is very cold, and it shines by reflecting sunlight.

As a comet approaches the fiery Sun it develops a coma, or halo. The Sun's wind and heat cause a long tail or two to stretch out far behind. Then the comet may be more than 100 million miles (160 million kilometers) long and can stretch halfway across the sky. A bright comet looks like a star with long hair trailing after it. Its name comes from an ancient word meaning ''long-haired.''

A comet may appear in the sky at any time. Some appear on predictable schedules. A spectacular comet may shine for weeks.

Comet Halley is the most famous. It has appeared in our sky every 75 years since at least 240 B.C. In

1985–1986 scientists from more than 50 countries used instruments on the ground and aboard spacecraft to gather more data than ever before. Comet Halley's nucleus measures about 9 by 5 miles (15 by 8 kilometers).

About five new comets are discovered every year, but you can't see most of them without a telescope.

gas tail

dust tail

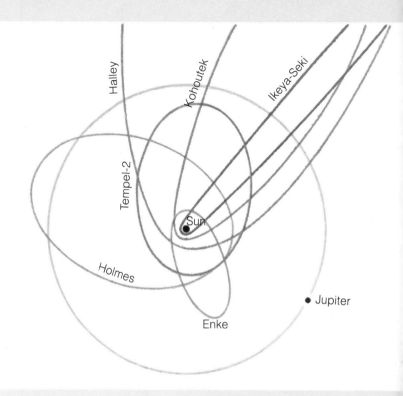

In the illustration above the paths of several comets are shown. If the comet rounds the Sun safely without breaking up, it heads back out to space. It freezes to a nucleus again. Each time a comet rounds the Sun, some gas and dust are left behind. After many passages the comet disintegrates.

When first seen in the distance, a comet looks like a faint blob of light. Then it brightens and grows a tail as it gets closer to the Sun.

A new comet is named by the first people to report it. Because there are comet hunters all over the world, comet names can be tongue-twisters. One famous example is the comet Honda-Mrkos-Pajdusakova.

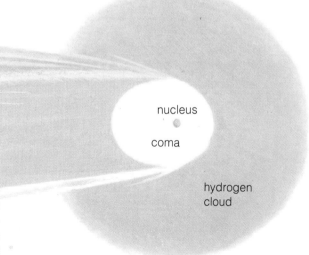

A comet's nucleus probably consists of frozen gases mixed with small solid particles. It is only a few miles (1 to 10 kilometers) wide. Surrounding the nucleus is the coma, which may stretch out for 60,000 miles (100,000 kilometers) or more. It contains dust that reflects sunlight and gases that fluoresce. A tail or two may extend for millions of miles into space. The tail is so thin that you can see stars through it. Comets are probably made out of the original material from which our solar system formed.

Meteors

A METEOR IS A streak of light made by a particle plunging through Earth's atmosphere and burning. A chunk of stone or metal that makes it through the air without burning up and then lands is called a meteorite. Meteorites are named for the post office that is nearest to the place where they land.

Fortunately most meteorites fall where no one lives. In one hundred years only about twenty to thirty have fallen near people. Injuries occur even less frequently, and there is no recorded case of anyone being killed.

Meteorites are valuable. Until rocks were brought back from the Moon, they were the only material from space that scientists could examine closely. A meteorite that fell near Murchison, Australia, in 1969 contained simple amino acids, the building blocks of all living things on Earth. Amino acids have also been found in meteorites collected in recent years in Antarctica, where they were well preserved. These finds indicate that the ingredients for living things exist in space and have led to speculation that life may too.

Big meteorites gouge out huge craters when they land on a planet or a moon. Craters caused by crashing meteorites have been found in many areas of the world. Fortunately our air blocks most meteorites. Mercury and our Moon have no air so they have many craters.

While stargazing, you may see occasional flashes of light. These "shooting stars" have nothing at all to do with real stars. They are meteors, the light trails of particles burning up as they zoom through our atmosphere at speeds of up to 45 miles (72 kilometers) per second. Meteors occur 48 to 60 miles (80 to 100 kilometers) above Earth; real stars are trillions of miles away.

Fireballs are especially bright meteors. They can glow spectacularly and be seen for miles.

Meteoroids are solid particles traveling in space. Many are left behind by comets that have returned to outer space. When Earth, moving in its orbit around the Sun, crosses a swarm of meteoroids, a meteor shower results. Then we see many meteors pouring

A meteoroid plunges through Earth's atmosphere.

down from one part of the sky. Meteor showers are named for the star group where they seem to originate.

A mysterious explosion occurred over Siberia in the Soviet Union in 1908. Its effects were felt all around the world. In the immediate area trees were blown down and charred. No craters have been found there, but Russian scientists figure that 4,000 tons of material fell to the ground either from a huge fireball or a comet. They found diamond-like grains and ashes in the area that looked like the remains of a meteorite fall.

The 66-ton Hoba West meteorite is the largest meteorite ever found. It is still where it fell in southwestern Africa.

WHEN AND WHERE TO LOOK FOR METEOR SHOWERS	
Date of Maximum	Constellation
April 23	Lyra
August 12	Perseus
October 21	Orion
November 16	Leo
December 13	Gemini

Barringer Crater, the meteorite crater in northern Arizona shown below, measures 4,150 feet (1,265 meters) wide and 570 feet (174 meters) deep. The object that dug this huge crater must have been traveling at more than 30,000 miles (48,000 kilometers) per hour.

The American Museum of Natural History in New York City has an exhibit containing the Ahnighito meteorite, which is the largest meteorite on display. It fell to Earth in Greenland and weighs 34 tons.

Humans in Space

IN 1961 DARING astronauts made the first journey into space. Scientists at first feared that the trips away from Earth might injure or even kill people.

Space travelers zoom from rest on the launch pad to a speed of 17,500 miles (28,000 kilometers) per hour in only a few minutes. Picking up speed that fast (accelerating), they feel a crushing force. Once in space, the travelers feel no force at all. They are apparently weightless. Day and night no longer occur every 24 hours. No air keeps away the broiling sunshine, freezing cold, deadly radiation, and meteoroids.

On its return the spacecraft rams into the atmosphere and its outside walls get flaming hot. Speed is lost so rapidly that the astronauts again feel crushed.

1. **First man in space:** Yuri Gagarin circled the Earth once in Vostok 1 on April 12, 1961, and then returned after 1 hour, 48 minutes.

First woman in space: Valentina V. Tereshkova completed 48 orbits in Vostok 6, June 16–19, 1963.

2. **First American in space:** Alan Shepard, on May 5, 1961. Flew for 15 minutes in Mercury capsule, Freedom 7.

First American in orbit: John H. Glenn, on February 20, 1962. Circled the Earth three times in Friendship 7.

3. **First spacewalk:** Alexei A. Leonov. Spent ten minutes outside Voskhod 2 in March 1965.

4. **First American spacewalk:** Edward H. White II. Glided for 20 minutes outside Gemini 4.

5. **First Soyuz test:** Vladimir M. Komarov, in April 1967. Orbited the Earth 17 times in Soyuz 1. After making a safe reentry, he was killed on landing.

6. **First man on the Moon:** Neil A. Armstrong, on July 20, 1969. Left the first human footprint on the Moon's surface.

7. **Longest time for Americans in space:** Skylab crew Gerald P. Carr, William R. Pogue, and Edward G. Gibson spent 84 days, 1 hour, and 16 minutes in space.

8. **Longest stay in space:** Leonard Kizim, Vladimir Solovyov, and Oleg Atkov spent 237 days in space aboard Salyut 7 in 1984.

9. **First international space mission:** Apollo and Soyuz docked in orbit in July 1975. Thomas P. Stafford, Vance D. Brand, and Donald K. Slayton visited with Alexei Leonov and Valery Kubasov.

10. **First reusable spacecraft:** Space shuttle Columbia, America's first reusable spacecraft, was launched April 12, 1981.

First American woman in space: Sally K. Ride was a mission specialist aboard Challenger, June 16–24, 1983.

For more than twenty years research has progressed toward longer and better space flights. Working separately, Americans and Russians designed capsules and spacesuits to seal astronauts into an environment like Earth's. They checked the breathing, heartbeat, temperature, and activities of astronauts in flight.

Later, astronauts docked, or linked up, with other craft in orbit. They photographed Earth and the Sun better than ever before. They put on spacesuits connected to lifelines and went outside their space vehicles to make repairs.

These brave pioneers proved that people can live and work in space for months. In the newer space vehicles experts from many countries can fly with the astronauts.

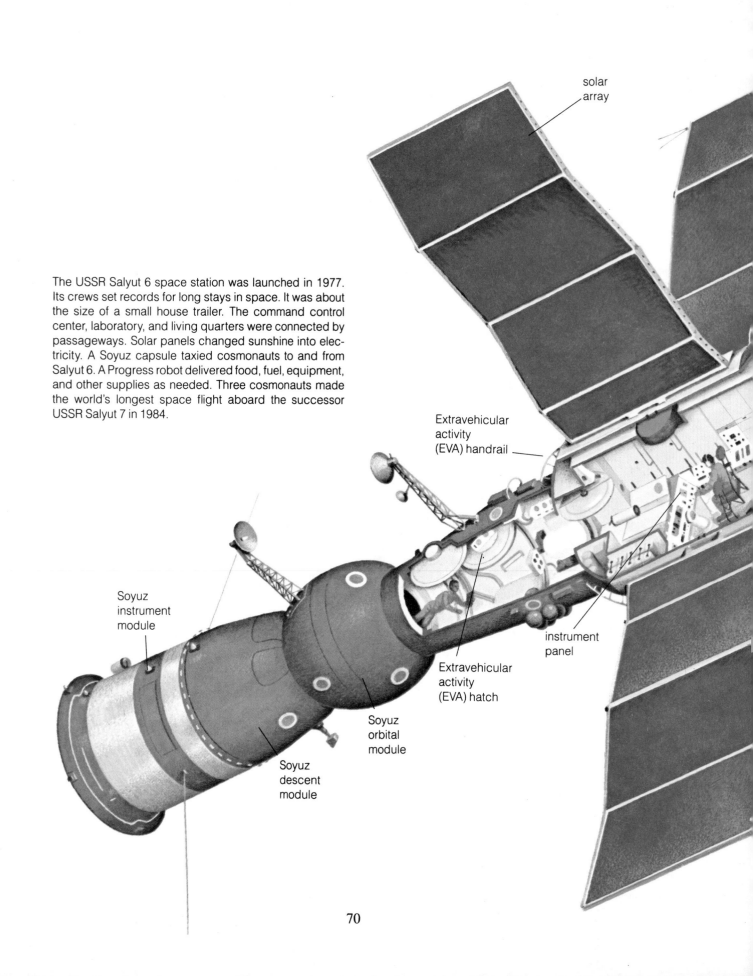

The USSR Salyut 6 space station was launched in 1977. Its crews set records for long stays in space. It was about the size of a small house trailer. The command control center, laboratory, and living quarters were connected by passageways. Solar panels changed sunshine into electricity. A Soyuz capsule taxied cosmonauts to and from Salyut 6. A Progress robot delivered food, fuel, equipment, and other supplies as needed. Three cosmonauts made the world's longest space flight aboard the successor USSR Salyut 7 in 1984.

solar array

Extravehicular activity (EVA) handrail

instrument panel

Extravehicular activity (EVA) hatch

Soyuz instrument module

Soyuz orbital module

Soyuz descent module

70

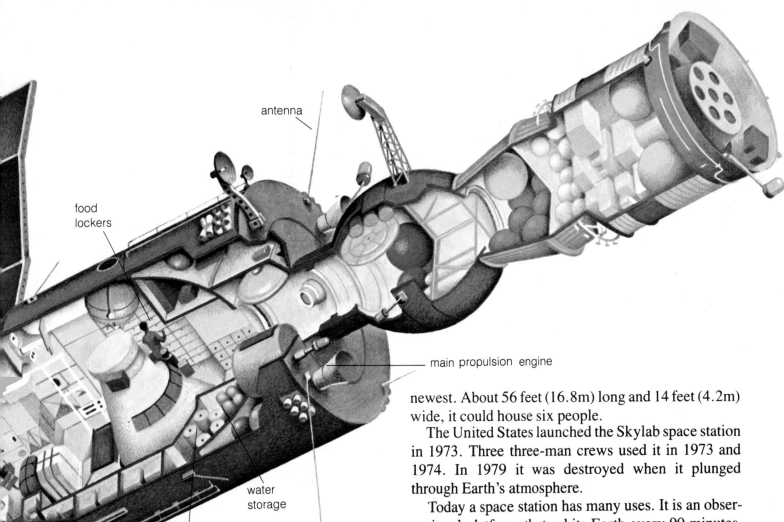

antenna

food lockers

main propulsion engine

water storage

refuse containers

Space Stations

A SPACE STATION is a structure that serves as a working place for humans while it orbits Earth above the atmosphere. Crews go there for specific missions and return to Earth when the work is done. They travel in a space capsule that docks with the station. Crews enter the space station through an airtight transfer compartment.

A life-support system aboard the space station provides air, comfortable temperatures, food, fresh water, and disposal of wastes. There are facilities for working, sleeping, recreation, and talking to people back home.

The USSR first orbited the Salyut 1 space station in 1971. Since then, improved space stations have been orbited and occupied by astronauts from different countries. The USSR Mir, launched in 1986, is the newest. About 56 feet (16.8m) long and 14 feet (4.2m) wide, it could house six people.

The United States launched the Skylab space station in 1973. Three three-man crews used it in 1973 and 1974. In 1979 it was destroyed when it plunged through Earth's atmosphere.

Today a space station has many uses. It is an observational platform that orbits Earth every 90 minutes. From it, crews can gather information about Earth's land, sea, and air. They can monitor forests and crops, trace pollution, map land and sea areas, prospect for oil and minerals, and watch for military activities.

It is an observatory. Telescopes can image the sun and distant stars without the atmospheric interference they encounter on Earth.

It is a biomedical laboratory for testing human endurance in space. Weightlessness and isolation can cause motion sickness, a loss of ability to concentrate, and irritability. After a month bones and muscles lose essential calcium and other minerals. Decalcified bones could break and a relaxed heart might fail when crews return to Earth after a long space flight. Space doctors hope to find out how food, exercise, and recreation can keep space travelers well on long missions.

It is a space research center for test-manufacturing of products such as new medicines and alloys in the zero-g and vacuum of space.

In the near future some space stations could be used as spaceports to launch spacecraft on flights to the planets or beyond. Others could be space factories for manufacturing products that can't be made on Earth.

SPACE SHUTTLE FACTS
(weights approximate)

LENGTH
   System: 184.2 ft (56.14 m)
   Orbiter: 122.2 ft (37.24 m)

HEIGHT
   System: 76.6 ft (23.34 m)
   Orbiter: 56.67 ft (17.27 m)

WINGSPAN
   Orbiter: 78.06 ft (23.79 m)

WEIGHT

GROSS LIFTOFF: 4.5 million lb (2,041,200 kg)

ORBITER LANDING: 212,000 lb (96,163 kg)
   (with payload)

THRUST
   Solid Rocket Boosters (SRB) (2):
      2.9 million lb (12,889,200 Newtons) of
      thrust each at sea level
   Orbiter Main Engines (3):
      375,000 lb (1,668,000 Newtons) of thrust
      each at sea level

CARGO BAY
   Dimensions: 60 ft long, 15 ft in diameter
      (18.28 m long, 4.57 m in diameter)
   Payloads: Unmanned spacecraft to fully
      equipped scientific laboratories

Space Shuttle

THE SPACE SHUTTLE is the world's first reusable spacecraft. A winged orbiter delivers people and equipment to Earth orbit for a mission, makes pickups, and then returns home.

The crew normally consists of a commander, a pilot, and a mission specialist, who are astronauts, and up to four payload specialists. The commander is responsible for mission operations and safety; the pilot is second in command. The mission specialist oversees payloads (cargo). Payload specialists take care of particular science experiments. They must be experts in their work but don't have to be astronauts.

The first step in becoming an astronaut is to be selected for training. Competition among hopefuls is tough. Astronauts must have a college degree in engineering, science, or mathematics and must be in excellent health. If they want to be pilots, they must also have experience flying jet aircraft.

Once selected to be an astronaut, a trainee has to learn more about basic science, space technology, and computers and stay in excellent physical condition by exercising regularly. Pilots must keep their flying skills sharp as well.

Astronauts must get used to living and working in the weightless condition (zero-g) they will experience in orbit. Simulators provide very realistic working conditions. Astronauts practice tasks while floating under water or flying "over the top" of a parabolic path in a jet aircraft.

A crew is assigned to a specific mission far in advance of the launch date. Several weeks before the scheduled flight a mission simulator is linked with mission control and simulated tracking stations. The crew and flight controllers practice the whole mission in a joint training exercise to make sure everything is ready for the real thing.

The orbiter may stay in space a few days or weeks.

At launch the orbiter lifts off, powered by three main engines and two solid rocket boosters. A large external tank feeds liquid hydrogen and oxygen to the main engines. After two minutes the solid rocket boosters are dropped. They parachute to the ocean for pickup and reuse. After eight minutes the empty external tank is abandoned over the ocean. The orbiter is powered into its path around Earth by two small engines.

Its velocity in orbit is about 17,500 miles (28,000 kilometers) per hour, circling Earth every 90 minutes.

Although the orbiter looks like an airplane, it is much more complex. It has 49 engines and 5 computers that argue actions among themselves. The cockpit has some 2,000 controls and displays for flying in space and air. Fuel cells containing hydrogen and oxygen generate electric power and also produce drinking water.

The crew lives and works in the cabin up front. The top level is the flight deck where the crew controls the orbiter and handles most payloads. Mid-deck is the living area where passengers eat, sleep, exercise, and take care of personal hygiene.

Payloads, in the large back area called the payload bay, may consist of communications, weather, and scientific or military intelligence satellites. Equipment can also be installed in the payload bay so the orbiter can serve as a space station. There is room for a pressurized modular space laboratory called Spacelab.

A robot arm over 50 feet (15 meters) long, operated by astronauts, reaches out from the orbiter. It has joints at the shoulder, elbow, and wrist, and a four-claw hand. It can take a satellite from the payload bay, set it in space, and release it to orbit on its own. It can also grab satellites that need repairs.

The orbiter has 23 antennas. Tracking stations give contact with mission control at the Johnson Space Center in Texas. When tracking and data relay satellites are in place in the mid-1980s, mission control will have almost continuous contact with orbiter crews.

When a shuttle is ready to return to Earth, crew members strap into their seats. The crew goes through a preburn checklist. Thruster rockets fire to slow the orbiter to allow it to drop out of orbit.

Fiery heat envelops the orbiter as it plunges through the atmosphere. Its heat shield can survive up to 3,000°F. (1,650°C.) during reentry.

The astronauts maneuver the shuttle like a glider in the air. They bring it to a landing traveling at about 215 miles (135 kilometers) per hour on a runway.

The orbiter is inspected and serviced. It is quickly readied for another flight.

Space Shuttle Mission Profile

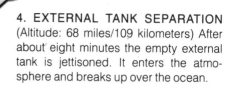

3. SOLID ROCKET BOOSTER SEPARATION (Altitude: 28 miles/45 kilometers) After about two minutes the solid rocket boosters are dropped. They parachute to the ocean for pickup and reuse.

4. EXTERNAL TANK SEPARATION (Altitude: 68 miles/109 kilometers) After about eight minutes the empty external tank is jettisoned. It enters the atmosphere and breaks up over the ocean.

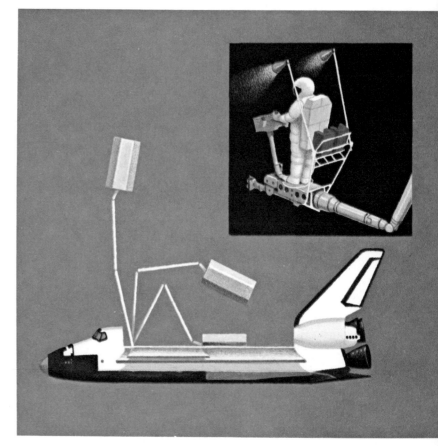

The remote manipulator system is a 50-foot (15-meter) arm that is remotely controlled. It can grapple payloads for deployment out of the orbiter cargo bay or catch them in space for return to Earth.

2. ASCENT The orbiter lifts off, powered by three main engines and two solid rocket boosters. A large external tank feeds liquid hydrogen and oxygen to the main engine.

10. GROUND After touchdown a ground crew does a safety inspection. Then the flight crew heads for a checkup, experiments go to scientists for study, and the orbiter is readied for another flight.

1. COUNTDOWN After entering the orbiter from the launch tower, the crew members lie on their backs, strapped into seats with their feet above their heads. Their systems checkout lasts about two hours.

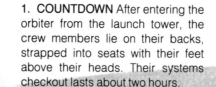

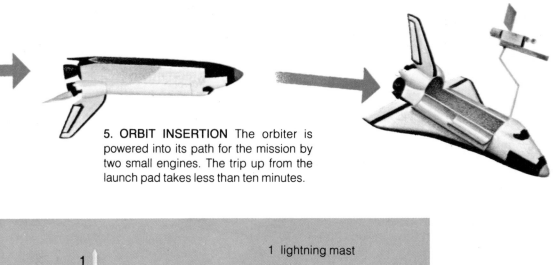

5. ORBIT INSERTION The orbiter is powered into its path for the mission by two small engines. The trip up from the launch pad takes less than ten minutes.

6. ORBITAL ACTIVITIES (Altitude: 115 to 690 miles/185 to 1,110 kilometers) The orbiter circles Earth, traveling at about 17,500 miles (28,000 kilometers) per hour. Cargo doors are opened. Missions last from a few days to weeks.

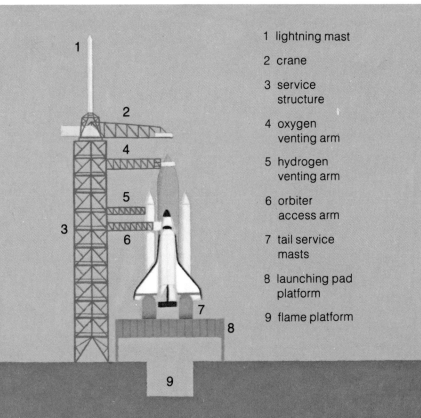

1 lightning mast

2 crane

3 service structure

4 oxygen venting arm

5 hydrogen venting arm

6 orbiter access arm

7 tail service masts

8 launching pad platform

9 flame platform

7. DEORBIT The cargo bay doors are closed. The crew straps into their seats. The orbiter reverses direction and fires engines for speed reduction.

8. REENTRY The orbiter rams into the atmosphere nose up so that the great heat produced hits its most protected parts.

9. LANDING The unpowered orbiter glides quickly to Earth in wide "S" curves. It lands like an airplane on a runway 15,000 feet (457 meters) long.

The speed brake, a flap at the rear of the rudder, helps slow the orbiter just before and during landing.

Fuel tanks for the maneuvering engines and thrusters.

The doors of the cargo bay are opened as soon as the spacecraft settles into orbit. They remain open most of the time that the orbiter is in space.

The long cargo bay carries a variety of payloads. There may be packages holding scientific experiments to be conducted in space. There may be up to five satellites to be lifted out and put into orbit. Or there may be a Spacelab module, a pressurized (air-filled) laboratory in which scientists can perform space-related experiments.

Three main engines burn for about eight minutes as the shuttle lifts off and then shut down for the rest of the mission.

Two maneuvering engines take over from the main engines and give the spacecraft its final push into orbit. They also supply energy to change orbits and to return to Earth.

Thrusters — small rockets — here and in the nose provide attitude (position) and orbit corrections when needed and also help control the orbiter during reentry.

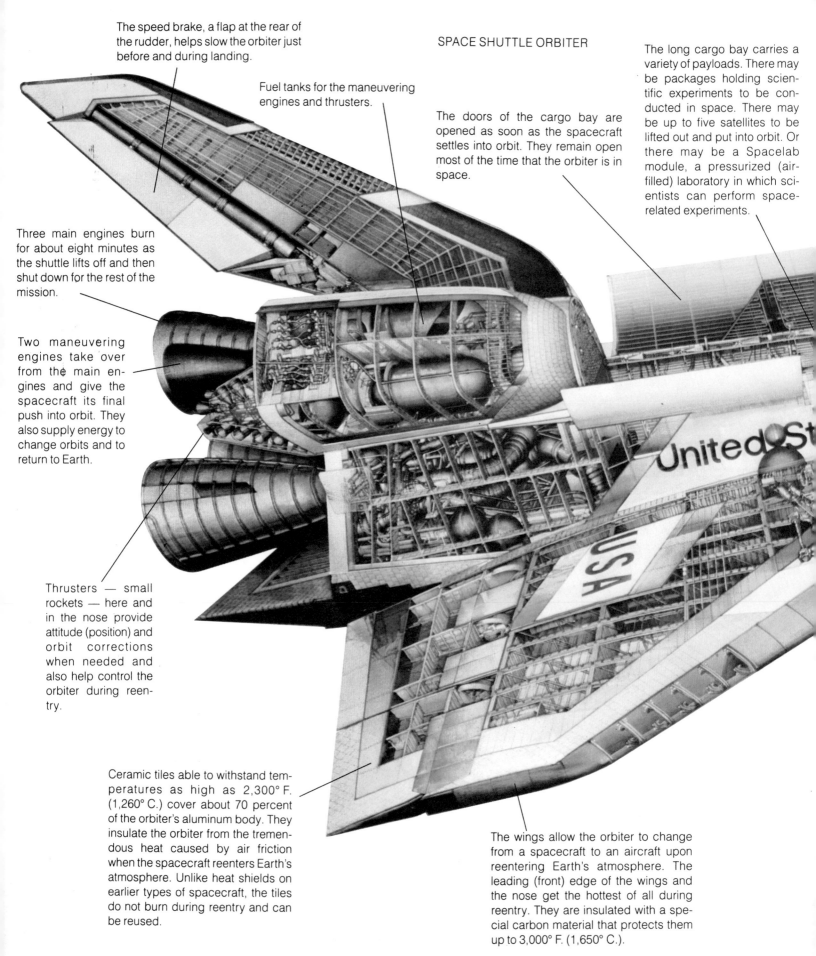

Ceramic tiles able to withstand temperatures as high as 2,300° F. (1,260° C.) cover about 70 percent of the orbiter's aluminum body. They insulate the orbiter from the tremendous heat caused by air friction when the spacecraft reenters Earth's atmosphere. Unlike heat shields on earlier types of spacecraft, the tiles do not burn during reentry and can be reused.

The wings allow the orbiter to change from a spacecraft to an aircraft upon reentering Earth's atmosphere. The leading (front) edge of the wings and the nose get the hottest of all during reentry. They are insulated with a special carbon material that protects them up to 3,000° F. (1,650° C.).

This payload is the LDEF (Long Duration Exposure Facility), a 30-foot-long canister in which the long-term effects of exposure to space can be tested on various instruments and materials. The LDEF is placed in orbit during one mission and is picked up months later by another.

The manipulator arm, which can move payloads in and out of the cargo bay, is controlled from the flight deck.

The pressurized cabin holds working and living quarters for the crew. It has an Earth-like atmosphere so that the crew members do not have to wear spacesuits while in orbit.

The flight deck of the cabin is the orbiter's work center. From here the crew controls the orbiter, handles most payloads, and runs many experiments. The flight deck can seat up to four people. An open hatch in the floor leads to the mid-deck below.

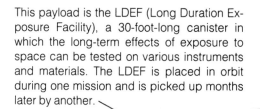

Thrusters

Nose gear

The mid-deck of the cabin is the crew's living area. It holds a galley (kitchen), bunks, hygiene station, lockers, and room for extra seats. An airlock at the rear lets a spacesuited astronaut pass from the air-filled cabin to the airless cargo bay.

Three fuel cells generate the electricity needed for everything from lights to computers to the manipulator arm. The cells also produce drinking water.

The main landing gear and the nose gear are lowered from the orbiter's body just before touchdown.

Astronauts in spacesuits can work outside the orbiter to make repairs and inspect equipment. They can also check on payloads in the cargo bay, perform experiments, and take photographs. A backpack worn over the suit provides oxygen and suit-cooling for up to six hours. The astronauts are tethered to the orbiter to keep them from floating off into space.

Astronauts can also wear a personal rocket kit called a manned maneuvering unit. Powered by jets of nitrogen gas, the rocket unit lets an astronaut do such outside work as assembling a space antenna or flying to a nearby satellite. The astronaut can remain tethered to the orbiter for safety.

Scorpius

Lepus

Ursa Major

Orion

Draco

Cygnus

Pegasus

Delphinus

Stargazing

WHEN YOU LOOK up in the sky on a clear, dark night, you can see about 2,000 stars. With a small telescope you can see hundreds of thousands more. Giant telescopes show billions.

As Earth travels around the Sun your view of the stars in outer space keeps changing. If you stargaze every month of the year, you can see more than 6,000 different stars as well as other interesting objects in the sky.

Stars seem to belong to groups called constellations. Stargazers often find groups that outline familiar things such as a baseball diamond or a triangle. In ancient times people divided the bright stars they saw into constellations, which they named after things they knew. Often these names were those of animals or heroes and heroines in their myths. The ancient peoples told stories about such constellations as Orion, the Hunter; Pegasus, the Winged Horse; and Ursa Major, the Great Bear.

Forty-eight constellations were recognized by the time of the famous Egyptian astronomer Ptolemy, who lived from A.D. 120 to about A.D. 180. More constellations were described later.

Today astronomers divide the sky into 88 sections, like geographers divide mainland United States into 48 states. The old constellation names now refer to these 88 sections instead of the mythical figures.

You can locate a star by referring to the constellation in which it appears. For example, noting that the star Betelgeuse is in Orion helps you find that red supergiant in the same way that knowing that Chicago is in Illinois helps you locate that city.

78

The brightest and best-known constellations visible from mid-northern latitudes are shown on the star maps in this book (pages 80–83). Constellation names are printed in capital letters.

You can observe that the Sun, Moon, and planets seem to move among twelve constellations during the year. These twelve are called the constellations of the zodiac. The ancients believed that these heavenly bodies were special. They developed astrology—the study of those bodies and their movements—in order to foretell how they supposedly influence human affairs.

Today this belt of constellations is still called the zodiac, but astronomers say that astrology has no scientific basis for foretelling the future.

Some constellations can be seen on every clear night all year. These are called circumpolar constellations. Look for them around Polaris, the North Star. Other constellations rise and set overnight and change with the seasons. You can use the star map that pictures the sky at the right time to help you when you stargaze.

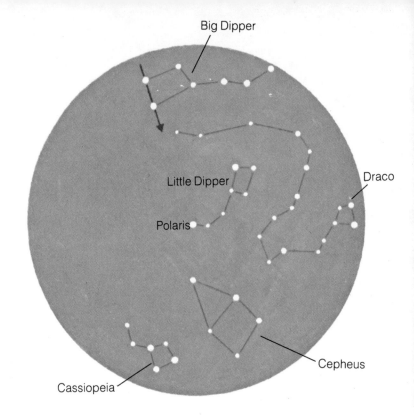

Above: The circumpolar stars visible from mid-northern latitudes are found around the polestar, Polaris, also called the North Star. "Circumpolar" means "surrounding the pole." As Earth turns during the night, you can see these stars move counterclockwise around Polaris. Below: The constellations of the zodiac.

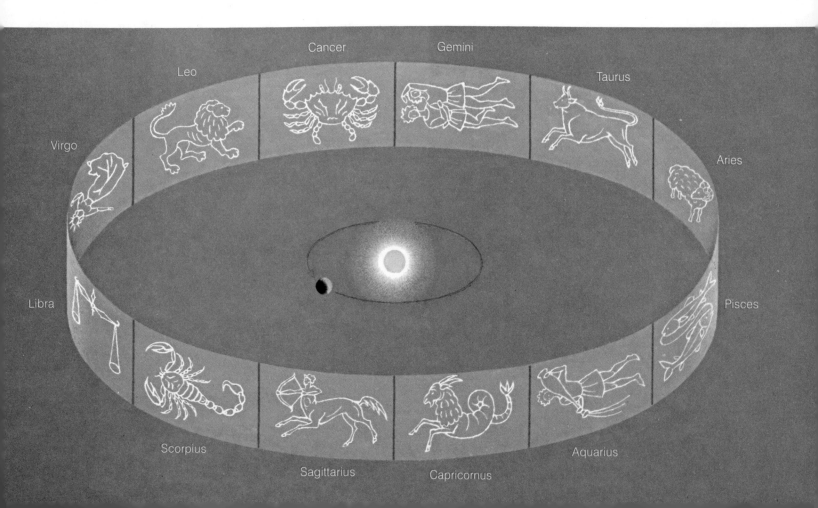

SPRING

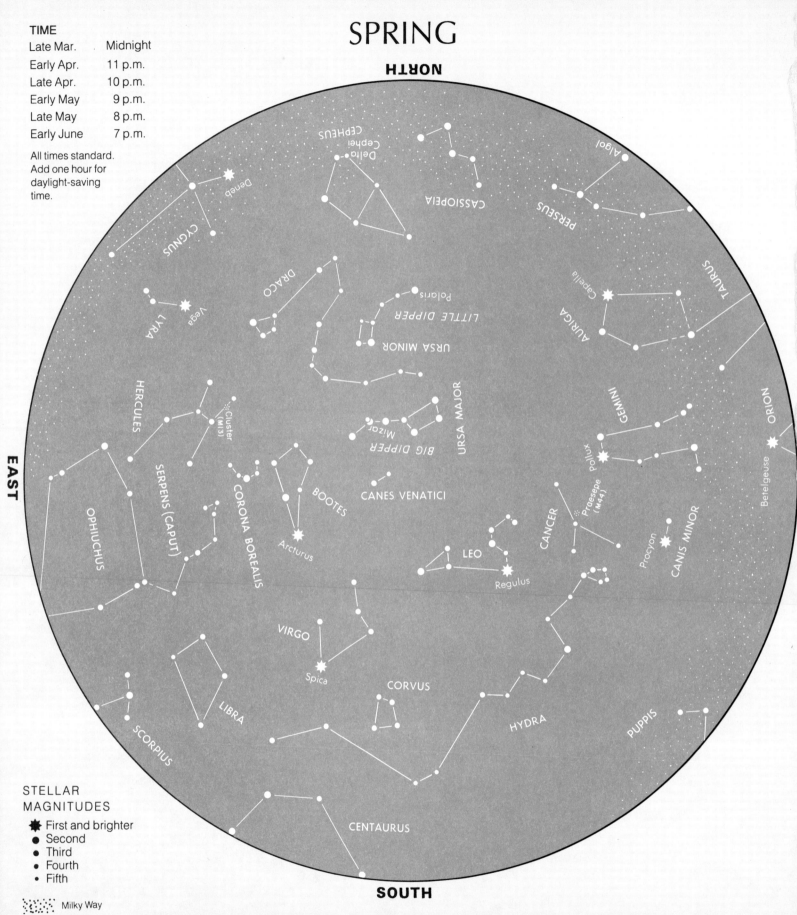

TIME

Late Mar.	Midnight
Early Apr.	11 p.m.
Late Apr.	10 p.m.
Early May	9 p.m.
Late May	8 p.m.
Early June	7 p.m.

All times standard.
Add one hour for
daylight-saving
time.

NORTH

EAST

SOUTH

CEPHEUS
Delta
Cephei
CASSIOPEIA
PERSEUS
Algol
Capella
TAURUS
DRACO
Polaris
LITTLE DIPPER
URSA MINOR
AURIGA
ORION
CYGNUS
Deneb
LYRA
Vega
HERCULES
Cluster
(M13)
URSA MAJOR
Mizar
BIG DIPPER
GEMINI
Pollux
Betelgeuse
SERPENS (CAPUT)
CORONA BOREALIS
BOOTES
CANES VENATICI
Praesepe
(M44)
CANCER
Procyon
CANIS MINOR
OPHIUCHUS
Arcturus
LEO
Regulus
VIRGO
Spica
CORVUS
HYDRA
PUPPIS
LIBRA
SCORPIUS
CENTAURUS

STELLAR MAGNITUDES

★ First and brighter
● Second
● Third
• Fourth
· Fifth

⠿ Milky Way

80

HOW TO USE THIS STAR MAP Turn this star map so that the direction you face matches the direction
you can read on the map. Identify the stars you see from your horizon up to the point overhead by
matching them with the constellation names you can read on the map. The stars on this map are visible
from mid-northern latitudes.

SUMMER

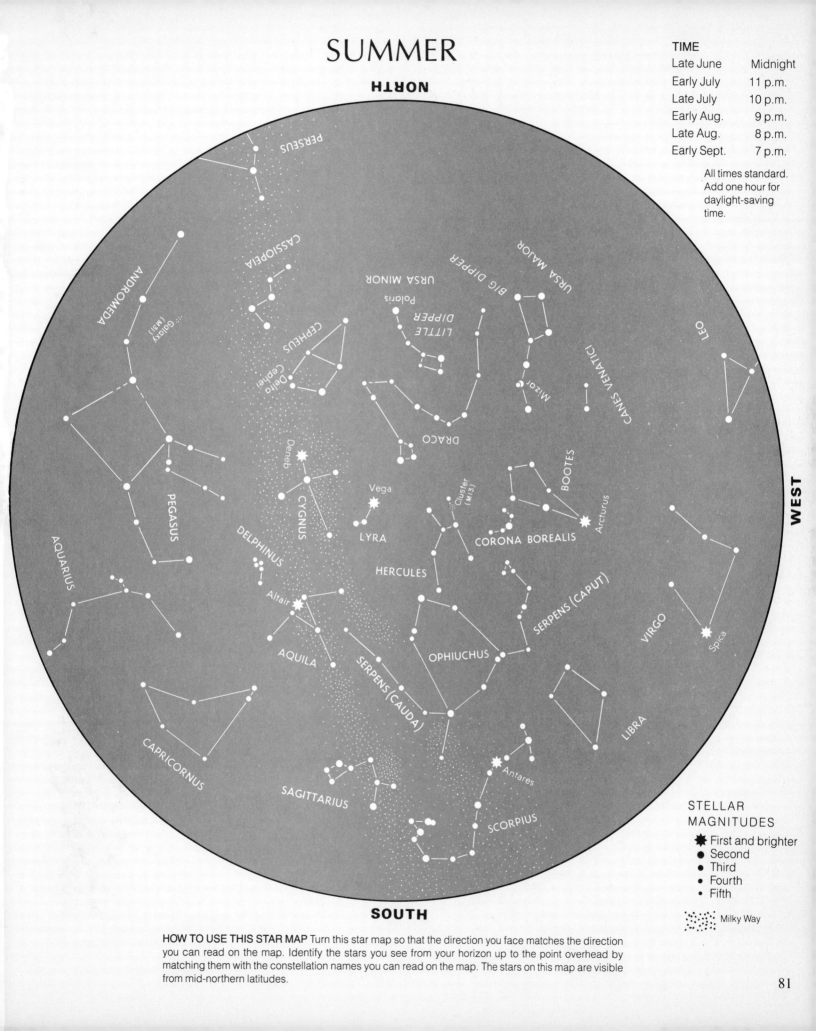

NORTH

PERSEUS

ANDROMEDA

CASSIOPEIA

Galaxy (M31)

CEPHEUS

Delta Cephei

URSA MINOR

Polaris

LITTLE DIPPER

BIG DIPPER

URSA MAJOR

LEO

PEGASUS

Deneb

CYGNUS

Vega

LYRA

Cluster (M13)

DRACO

Mizar

CANES VENATICI

BOOTES

Arcturus

AQUARIUS

DELPHINUS

HERCULES

CORONA BOREALIS

SERPENS (CAPUT)

VIRGO

Spica

Altair

AQUILA

SERPENS (CAUDA)

OPHIUCHUS

LIBRA

CAPRICORNUS

SAGITTARIUS

Antares

SCORPIUS

SOUTH

WEST

TIME

Late June	Midnight
Early July	11 p.m.
Late July	10 p.m.
Early Aug.	9 p.m.
Late Aug.	8 p.m.
Early Sept.	7 p.m.

All times standard. Add one hour for daylight-saving time.

STELLAR MAGNITUDES

✦ First and brighter
● Second
● Third
• Fourth
· Fifth

⋰⋱ Milky Way

HOW TO USE THIS STAR MAP Turn this star map so that the direction you face matches the direction you can read on the map. Identify the stars you see from your horizon up to the point overhead by matching them with the constellation names you can read on the map. The stars on this map are visible from mid-northern latitudes.

81

AUTUMN

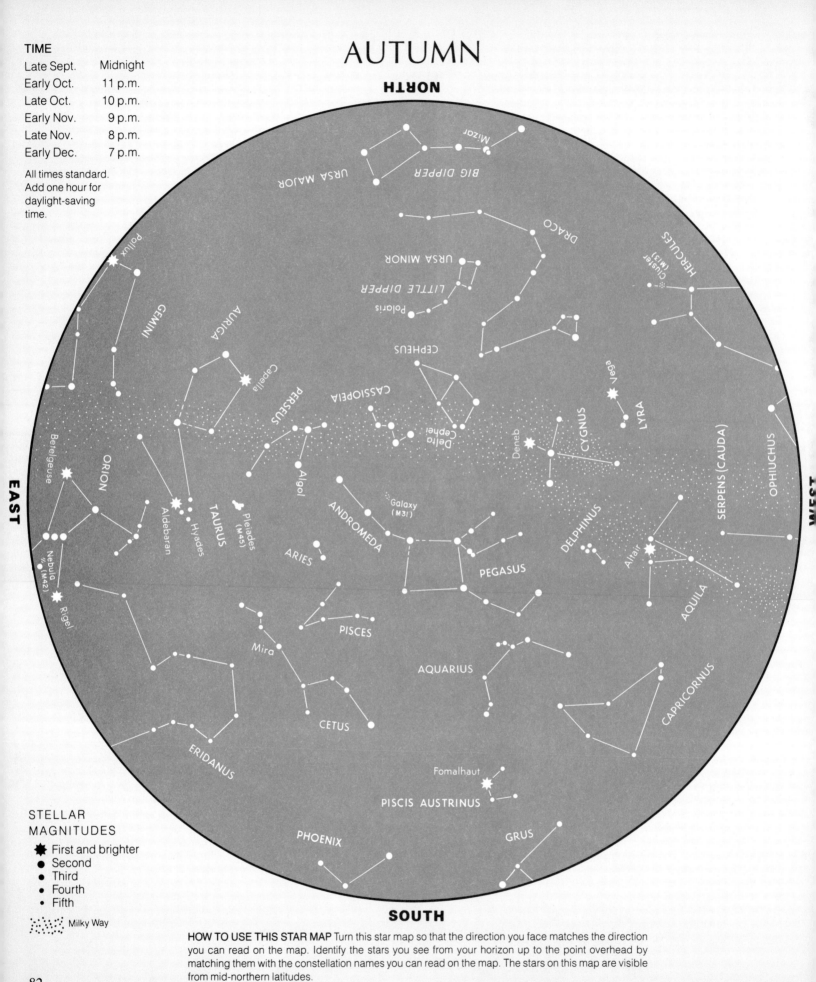

TIME

Late Sept.	Midnight
Early Oct.	11 p.m.
Late Oct.	10 p.m.
Early Nov.	9 p.m.
Late Nov.	8 p.m.
Early Dec.	7 p.m.

All times standard. Add one hour for daylight-saving time.

STELLAR MAGNITUDES

- ✶ First and brighter
- ● Second
- • Third
- • Fourth
- · Fifth

⠿ Milky Way

HOW TO USE THIS STAR MAP Turn this star map so that the direction you face matches the direction you can read on the map. Identify the stars you see from your horizon up to the point overhead by matching them with the constellation names you can read on the map. The stars on this map are visible from mid-northern latitudes.

WINTER

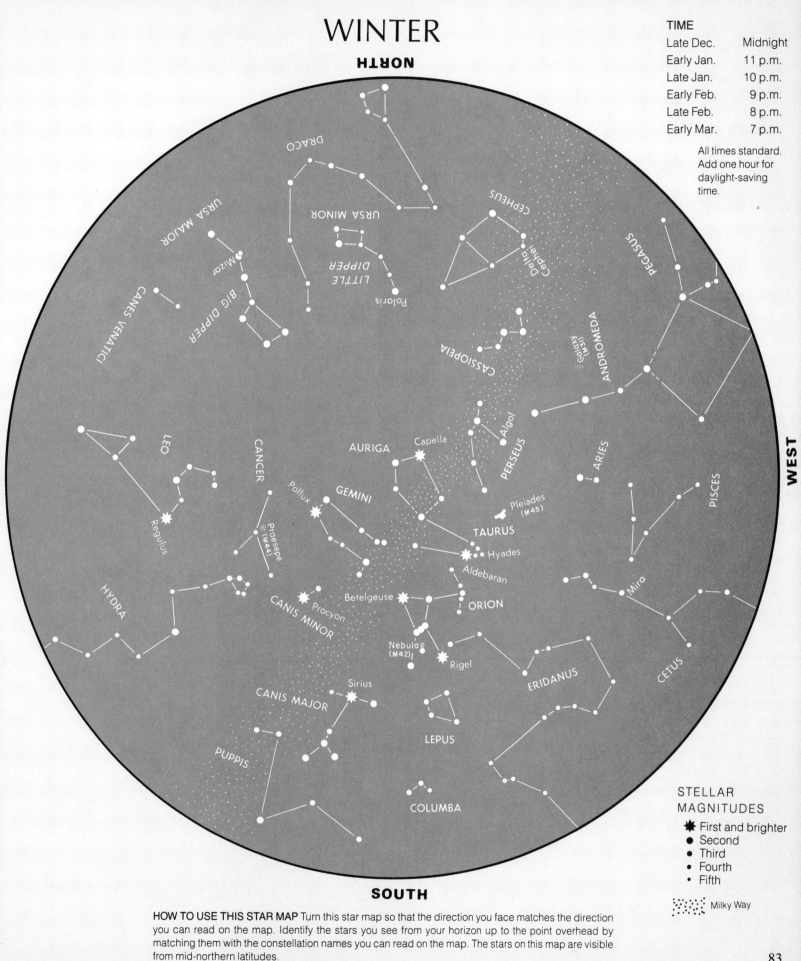

NORTH

DRACO

URSA MINOR

URSA MAJOR

Mizar

BIG DIPPER

LITTLE DIPPER

Polaris

CANES VENATICI

CEPHEUS

Delta Cephei

PEGASUS

CASSIOPEIA

ANDROMEDA

Galaxy (M31)

PERSEUS

Algol

ARIES

PISCES

LEO

CANCER

AURIGA

Capella

GEMINI

Pollux

Praesepe (M44)

Regulus

Procyon

CANIS MINOR

Betelgeuse

ORION

Pleiades (M45)

TAURUS

Hyades

Aldebaran

Mira

HYDRA

CANIS MAJOR

Sirius

Nebula (M42)

Rigel

LEPUS

ERIDANUS

CETUS

PUPPIS

COLUMBA

SOUTH

WEST

TIME

Late Dec.	Midnight
Early Jan.	11 p.m.
Late Jan.	10 p.m.
Early Feb.	9 p.m.
Late Feb.	8 p.m.
Early Mar.	7 p.m.

All times standard. Add one hour for daylight-saving time.

STELLAR MAGNITUDES

✦ First and brighter
● Second
• Third
· Fourth
· Fifth

⣿ Milky Way

HOW TO USE THIS STAR MAP Turn this star map so that the direction you face matches the direction you can read on the map. Identify the stars you see from your horizon up to the point overhead by matching them with the constellation names you can read on the map. The stars on this map are visible from mid-northern latitudes.

Stars

THE STARS THAT you see at night are huge, hot, shining balls of gas like our Sun. Some are much bigger than the Sun. They look like tiny lights because they are trillions of miles from Earth.

The closest star to Earth is the Sun; the next closest star is called Proxima Centauri. No one can see Proxima Centauri without the aid of a telescope. The closest star that is visible (except for the Sun) is Alpha Centauri. Alpha Centauri cannot be seen from mid-northern latitudes, so it is not on the star maps.

Sirius, in the constellation Canis Major (the Great Dog), is the brightest and closest nighttime star that can be seen from mid-northern latitudes. It is almost 9 light-years from Earth. This means that if you could travel in a spacecraft at the speed of light, it would take you almost 9 years to reach Sirius. At the same speed you would travel about 8 minutes to reach the Sun, 4.3 years to reach Proxima Centauri, 4.5 years to reach Alpha Centauri, and 782 years to reach Polaris, the North Star.

The constellations that you see in the sky will seem to stay the same for your entire lifetime. But all these stars are actually moving. Most of them have speeds of hundreds of miles per hour. For example, the Sun is racing toward the constellation Hercules at 45,000 miles (72,000 kilometers) per hour, taking Earth and the other planets with it. The stars are so far away that we cannot notice their positional changes made in a short period of time. If you could return to Earth thousands of years from now, you would see many changes.

Like our Sun, the other stars produce their own light by nuclear fusion reactions in their centers. If you look at stars very carefully, you will see that they are different colors. Their colors are the result of different temperatures, even though all stars are extremely hot.

The hottest stars that you can see are blue-white. Their surface temperature is over 19,000° F. (10,000° C.). Yellow stars like the Sun are medium

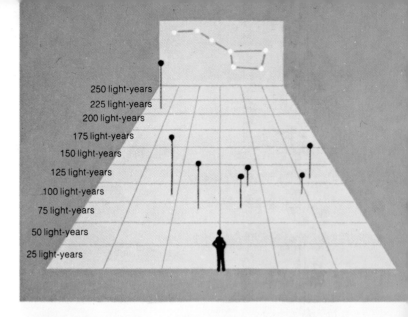

All of the stars in a group such as the Big Dipper look as if they belong together and are about the same distance from us, but they are really far apart at different distances from Earth. In the diagram above each dot stands for a star. The numeral beside it indicates the number of light-years away from Earth that star is.

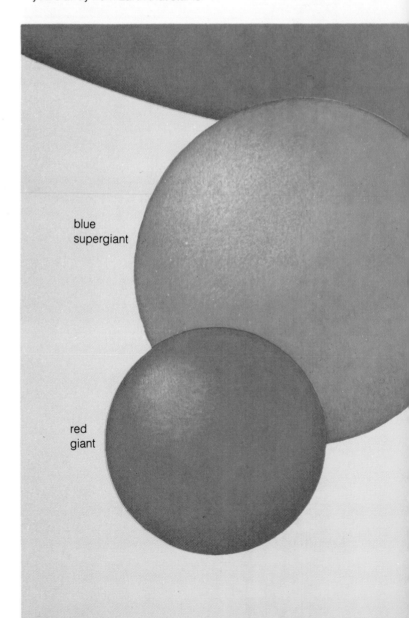

blue supergiant

red giant

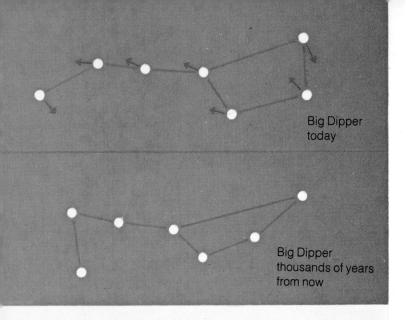

Big Dipper
today

Big Dipper
thousands of years
from now

The positions of the stars definitely do change over a period of time, although these periods of time are long ones. All of the stars are in motion and are not necessarily moving in the same direction. Over a period of thousands of years the pattern of the Big Dipper, for example, will be quite different.

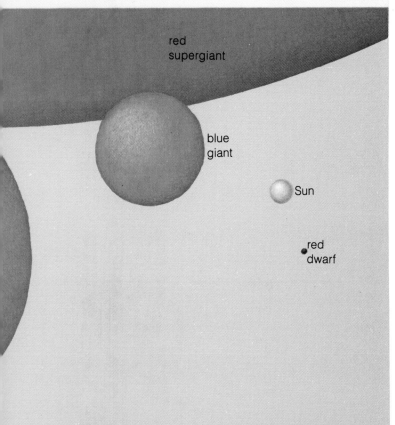

red
supergiant

blue
giant

Sun

red
dwarf

The sizes of the various stars can vary greatly. The width of the Sun, for example, is 109 times greater than the width of Earth. Some of the supergiant stars are many thousands of times wider than Earth. On the other hand, the common red dwarf stars may be not much wider than Earth.

hot. The coolest stars you can see are red. Their surface temperature is about 3,500° F. (2,000° C.).

Ancient astronomers observed that some stars are very bright and others are faint. The Greek astronomer Hipparchus, who lived in the second century B.C., put together a catalog of about a thousand stars. He divided them into six categories according to how bright they looked. The brightest stars were ranked as first magnitude and the faintest as sixth magnitude.

Today star magnitudes are based upon precise measurements with photometers (devices that measure the intensity of light instead of eye estimates of their brightness). The measurement of how bright a star looks is called its apparent magnitude, and this is shown by a symbol on the star maps. The brighter a star looks to us, the lower its magnitude number.

Sirius, next to the Sun the brightest star we can see, has a magnitude of −1.5. Bright stars, such as Vega in Lyra, have a magnitude of 0. The next brightest, such as Spica in Virgo, have a magnitude of 1. The faintest stars that you can see with the naked eye under the best conditions are about magnitude 6. Because it is so close to us, the Sun has an apparent magnitude of −27.

You cannot tell just by looking at the stars which ones are shining the most starlight into space. The Sun, for example, looks many times brighter than the other stars, but it is not. How bright a star looks depends not only on how much light it sends out but also on how far it is from Earth. The Sun looks so extraordinarily bright because it is hundreds of thousands of times closer to us than any other star.

A star's actual rate of sending out light is called its luminosity. The Sun shines as much as 3,830 billion trillion 100-watt light bulbs together. A few superluminous stars are a million times brighter than the Sun. Red dwarf stars are less than 1/2000 as bright. If two stars differ by one unit of magnitude, the brighter one is 2.5 times more luminous than the other.

H–R Diagrams, Binaries, and Variables

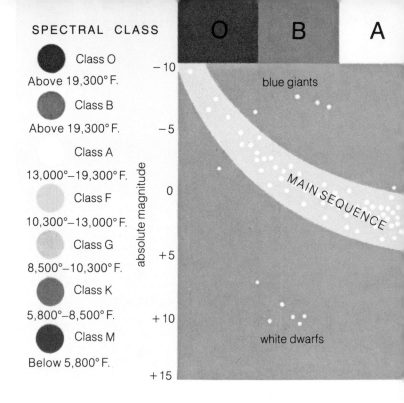

SPECTRAL CLASS			
Class O			
Above 19,300° F.			
Class B			
Above 19,300° F.			
Class A			
13,000°–19,300° F.			
Class F			
10,300°–13,000° F.			
Class G			
8,500°–10,300° F.			
Class K			
5,800°–8,500° F.			
Class M			
Below 5,800° F.			

H-R (Hertzsprung-Russell) diagrams chart the luminosity, temperature, absolute magnitude, and spectral class of stars. Each circle on an H-R diagram stands for a star. The ones with the highest luminosity are at the top. The highest temperature is toward the left.

THE MEASUREMENT OF the amounts of light that stars give off is called absolute magnitude. The measurement of how bright a star looks is called its apparent magnitude. The difference between a star's apparent magnitude and its absolute magnitude indicates the star's distance from Earth.

The brighter a star looks to us, the lower its apparent magnitude number. The brightest star, Sirius, has a magnitude of −1.5. The faintest stars you can see under the best conditions are about magnitude 6. Our Sun has an apparent magnitude of −27 because it is so close to us.

The Danish astronomer Ejnar Hertzsprung (1873–1967) and the American astronomer Henry Norris Russell (1877–1957) compared many stars to see how they were alike and how they differed.

Between 1911 and 1913 their results were pictured in what is called the Hertzsprung–Russell, or H–R, diagram. Astronomers today use H–R diagrams as a guide for their theories about stars.

Most stars are positioned along a track called the main sequence, which runs from the upper left to the lower right of the H–R diagram. Big, hot stars appear at the top left and shine the brightest. Yellow stars, such as our Sun, are placed in the center. The red dwarfs at the bottom right are the most common type of star in our part of space. They are small, cool, and faint.

Blue supergiants, such as Rigel in Orion, are the hottest bright stars of all. Red supergiants, such as Betelgeuse in Orion, and orange giants, such as Arcturus in Boötes, are cool but very luminous, mainly because they are so huge. Betelgeuse is so big that millions of stars the size of the Sun would fit inside it. White dwarf stars are extremely hot. However, they are faint because they are small.

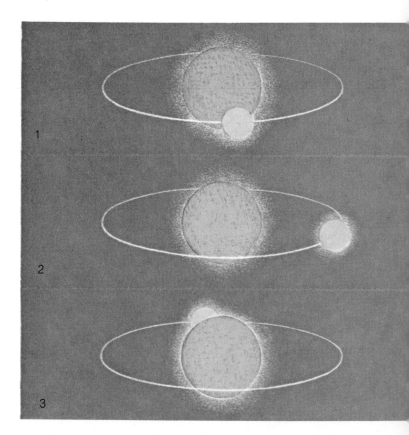

Eclipsing binaries vary in brightness. In 1 the brighter star eclipses the fainter star. In 2 the stars shine together, and in 3 the larger star blocks the light of the brighter star.

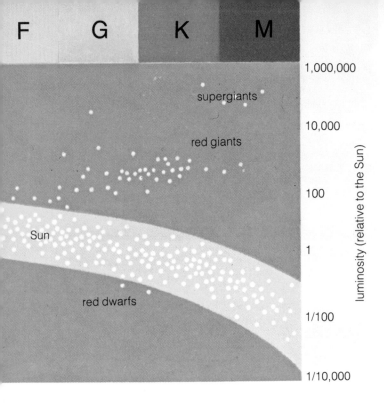

When a few thousand stars are chosen by chance and plotted on this diagram, they fall into certain patterns. This pattern suggests that there is a real connection between star luminosity and temperature. If this were not so, the dots would be scattered all over the chart.

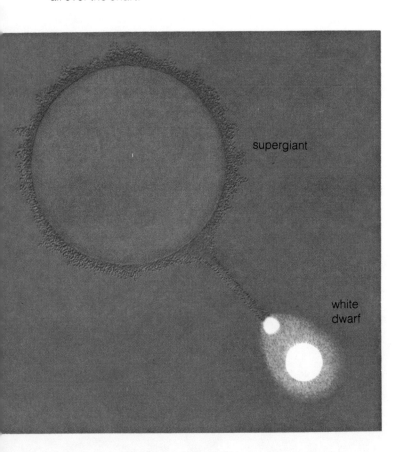

There can be an exchange of mass between the two parts of a binary star, as in this case of a supergiant and a white dwarf. When mass of the companion star falls onto the white dwarf, a nova is produced.

Many stars that look single really have one or more companions. Binary stars are two stars that are bound together by gravity and revolve around a common point while they travel through space.

A visual binary can be seen as two separate stars through a telescope. Italian astronomer Giovanni Riccioli was the first to recognize a visual binary. In 1650 his telescope separated Mizar in the handle of the Big Dipper into two separate stars.

If a binary system is located so that the stars block each other's light from our view as they revolve, it is called an eclipsing binary. You can observe the star Algol in Perseus change regularly in brightness in about three days.

William Herschel (1738–1822) and his sister, Caroline Herschel (1750–1848), carefully observed many binary star systems. They thought that many pairs of stars were associated with each other by gravitational forces that made them move in orbits around a common point. When they saw these orbital motions, they proved that Newton's law of gravitation operates outside our own solar system.

Most stars in our galaxy shine steadily, but more than 20,000 stars are called variables because their light output changes. Over half are pulsating variable stars that change periodically in size and brightness. Red variables take months or years between their brightest and faintest periods. It is interesting to observe the famous variable red supergiant Mira in Cetus. Because Mira changes from its maximum bright red to invisible, it was nicknamed "The Wonderful." Shorter period stars, such as the Cepheid variables, are less common but are important because their light output is used to measure distances in space. You can see the first known Cepheid variable, delta Cephei. It was discovered in 1784 by the teenage English astronomer John Goodricke two years before he died at the age of 21.

Eruptive variables are stars that suddenly shine brilliantly. A nova is a star that may temporarily blaze millions of times brighter than usual. Novas keep their form and most of their substance after their outburst and may flare again without warning.

Evolution of Stars

THE BRIGHT STARS IN space look the same today as they did hundreds and thousands of years ago when they were named by the ancients. Nobody lives long enough to see stars change, but astronomers say that they do change, over eons.

The most popular theory is that stars are born in huge swirling nebulas, or clouds, in space. These clouds have random lumps in which gas and dust particles fly together briefly. Their gravity pulls in more and more nearby gas and dust. The spinning globule grows bigger and bigger. Such globules can gather enough material to form many stars like our Sun.

A very massive globule slowly collapses under its own weight. Its center gets hotter and more dense. When the heat flows from the center to the surface, the globule glows deep red. Several millions of years later the temperatures inside reach 18,000,000° F. (10,000,000° C.).

At that temperature nuclear fusion reactions begin. Groups of four hydrogen nuclei are fused into single lighter helium nuclei. At the same time tremendous amounts of energy are released. Albert Einstein (1879–1955) described the energy released in his famous equation, $E = mc^2$. E stands for the energy released, m is the mass lost, and c is the speed of light.

When the outward pressure of the hot gases balances the star's weight, the collapse stops. Energy produced in the core eventually reaches the surface of the star, and the star shines. It gives off its own light steadily for millions or billions of years during what is called the star's main sequence period.

About 5 billion years ago our Sun was born in such a process. Its formation took about 30 million years. Much less massive stars may take 100 million years to light up.

Our Sun has been shining steadily since its birth. So much energy is released in each nuclear fusion reaction that only a small fraction of the Sun's hydrogen fuel changes to sunshine over a billion years. The Sun should continue to shine for another 5 billion years.

The death of a star begins when its hydrogen fuel is

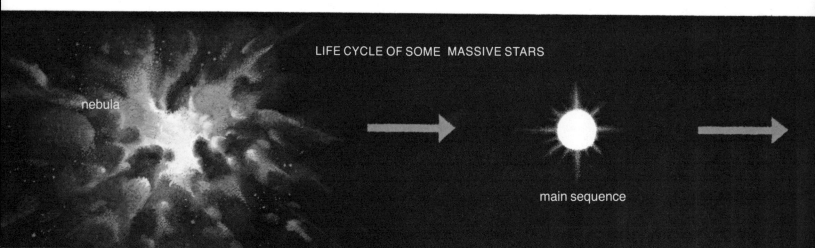

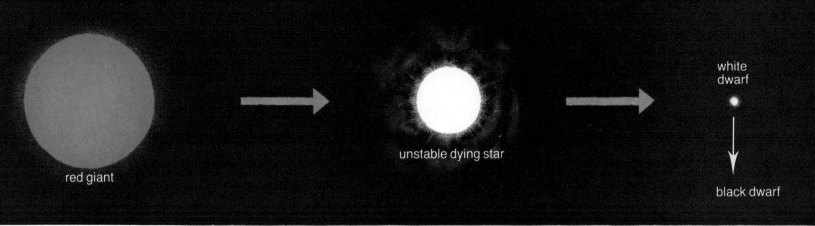

red giant

unstable dying star

white dwarf

black dwarf

finally used up. Then the star begins to swell to an enormous size. Its surface gradually cools and it starts to glow red. That gigantic red star is called a red giant. In about 5 billion more years the Sun should become a red giant, swelling out past Mercury, Venus, Earth, and Mars. All stars finally die.

As the life cycle of a solar-type star continues, it becomes unstable and throws off a shell of gas called a planetary nebula. After that it collapses to a super-dense star about the size of Earth, called a white dwarf. Slowly the white dwarf gives off its last light and eventually goes out. All that remains in space is a cold, dark black dwarf star.

Extremely massive red giant stars undergo more contractions and expansions, which raise their core temperature, pressure, and density. Their nuclear fires create elements such as carbon, nitrogen, and oxygen. After the fusion of iron occurs, they collapse finally. Some of these explode violently. They are called supernovas and may shine like billions of suns.

Supernovas produce the heaviest elements, such as silver, gold, and uranium. A supernova hurls mate-

rials far out into space, where they may contribute to the formation of new stars and planets. After its death a supernova may leave behind a dense corpse, called a neutron star, which is about ten miles wide and has more mass than the Sun.

A pulsar, or pulsating radio star, emits regular radio signals or pulses. Pulsars are evidently magnetized neutron stars that are rotating rapidly.

A neutron star may continue to collapse and form a tiny superdense dead star called a black hole. If black holes do exist, no one can ever see them. Their gravity is so strong that nothing, not even light, can escape from them.

Astronomers look for black holes indirectly. A black hole may pull in matter from a nearby visible star. Gas disappearing over the black hole's edge may send out bursts of X rays that can be detected. Cygnus X-1 is a binary star system that sends out bursts of X rays and seems to match this description. The invisible member's mass is more than eight times greater than the Sun's. It may be the first black hole ever detected.

red giant

supernova

neutron star

possible black hole

The Milky Way Galaxy

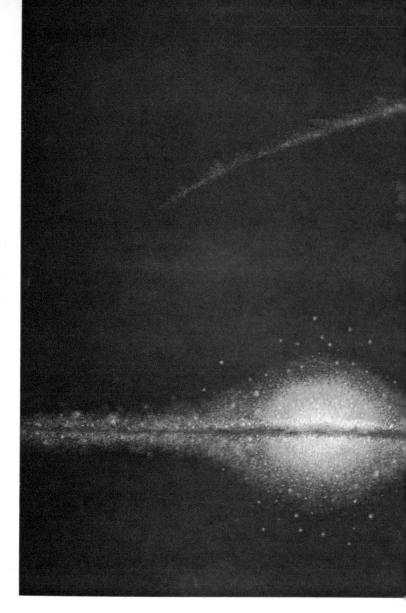

EARTH, THE SUN, AND all the stars you see at night belong to a gigantic star system called the Milky Way Galaxy. There are gas, dust, and more than 100 billion stars in the Milky Way Galaxy. They are all held together by the force of gravity as our Galaxy moves in space.

The most popular theory is that the Milky Way Galaxy formed more than 12 billion years ago from a colossal swirling cloud of hydrogen and helium. Its spinning flattened the Galaxy into an enormous disk surrounded by a faint halo of old star groups.

From far out in space the Milky Way Galaxy must now look like a huge sparkling phonograph record with most of its stars shining in a spiral pattern around the "grooves." A starry nucleus bulges in the middle like a swollen label.

The Milky Way Galaxy measures 100,000 light-years across and up to 2,000 light-years thick. If a spacecraft could move at the speed of light, it would have to travel 100,000 years to get from one side to the other.

The whole Galaxy spins slowly in space. Like a speck of dust on an ordinary record, our solar system goes along. It takes roughly 200 million years to go once around the center of the Galaxy. We have barely completed a circuit since dinosaurs lived on Earth.

Many stars in the Milky Way Galaxy belong to groups called clusters that stay together. In the spiral arms are open clusters containing up to 1,000 stars. Stars in the open clusters are relatively young. In the halo are globular clusters with up to a million stars. They are some of the oldest stars in our Galaxy.

The stars in the Milky Way Galaxy are far apart from each other. A star's nearest neighbor, on the average, is 5 light-years away. For a comparison, if you used basketballs to represent the stars, you would have to put them about 5,000 miles (8,000 kilometers) apart to represent the distance.

The space between the stars is almost empty. Hydrogen is the most abundant material, and there are some extremely tiny dust particles. Most of the gas and dust is in the spiral arms. Here new stars are born.

Astronomers have found over 50 different materials in the nebulas of the Milky Way Galaxy. Among them are water vapor and organic molecules. These are the basic ingredients of all living things on Earth. Perhaps there are other solar systems and living things in our Galaxy too.

Dust clouds block even the biggest optical telescopes from a view far into the Milky Way Galaxy. Today radio, infrared, and high-energy telescopes are adding much to our knowledge of the Galaxy in which we live.

The Milky Way Galaxy is a spiral galaxy. Earth, with everybody on it, circles the Sun about 30,000 light-years from the center of the Galaxy. The illustration above shows a top and side view of our Galaxy.

16.6 light-years   van Maanen's · 13.9 light-years   Procyon · 11.4 light-years   61 Cygni · 11.2 light-years   Sirius · 8.6 light-years   Barnard's · 5.9 light-years   Alpha Centauri · 4.3 light-years   Sun

A globular cluster (right) may have up to a million stars. The diagram shows some of the stars that are closest to Earth.

Elliptical galaxies are round to flattened pancake-shaped in appearance.

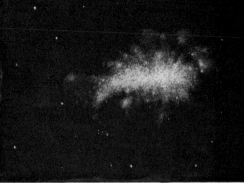

The brilliant arms of a spiral galaxy radiate out from the nucleus and trail through a disk, surrounded by a faint halo.

Irregular galaxies have no regular shape.

Neighboring Galaxies

MORE THAN 200 YEARS ago telescopes showed astronomers faint "nebulas" in the dark sky. Philosopher Immanuel Kant (1724–1804) and astronomer William Herschel (1738–1822) speculated that some of the "nebulas" were distant islands of stars beyond our Galaxy. Others disagreed. Until the twentieth century the Milky Way Galaxy was the only star system that was recognized.

American astronomer Edwin Hubble (1889–1953) settled the controversy in 1924. He photographed the "nebulas" through the largest telescope available at the time—the 100-inch (254-centimeter) telescope on Mount Wilson in California. He proved that many of them were star systems, or galaxies far beyond ours.

A galaxy is gas, dust, and a group of millions or billions of stars held together by the force of gravity. Powerful telescopes today record billions of galaxies in all directions in space. The universe may have 100 billion galaxies, each typically containing some 100 billion stars.

Galaxies occur in three basic shapes: spiral, ellipti-

cal, and irregular. Like our Milky Way Galaxy, other spiral galaxies contain large amounts of gas and dust in their disks. They are made up of young, middle-aged, and old stars. Elliptical galaxies seem to contain only old stars. Most irregular galaxies contain chiefly bright young stars, some old stars, and large amounts of gas and dust.

Most of the galaxies seem to belong to groups called clusters of galaxies. These clusters are held together by their tremendous gravitational attractions as they spin in space. Our Milky Way Galaxy belongs to a cluster called the Local Group. The Local Group contains more than 20 galaxies in a great sphere that is 3 million light-years across.

There are thousands of other clusters of galaxies that contain over 1,000 galaxies. These are called rich clusters. The closest rich cluster is in Virgo, about 62 million light-years from Earth. It consists of about 2,500 galaxies.

Superclusters are the largest known formations in the universe. A supercluster is a cluster of clusters of

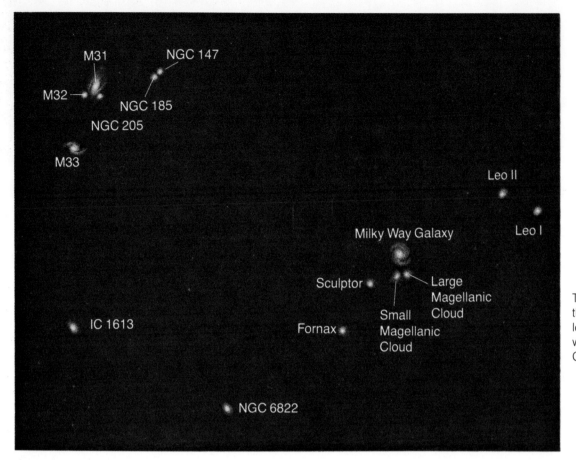

M31

NGC 147

M32

NGC 185

NGC 205

M33

Leo II

Leo I

Milky Way Galaxy

Sculptor

Large Magellanic Cloud

Small Magellanic Cloud

IC 1613

Fornax

NGC 6822

The Local Group. Earth belongs to the solar system, which in turn belongs to the Milky Way Galaxy, which in turn belongs to the Local Group of more than 20 galaxies.

galaxies. Our solar system belongs to the Milky Way Galaxy; the Milky Way Galaxy belongs to the Local Group; and the Local Group, in turn, belongs to the Virgo supercluster, which is several hundred million light-years across.

Because they send out extraordinarily large amounts of energy, some galaxies are called peculiar.

All galaxies send out radio signals. Peculiar radio galaxies are extremely bright at radio wavelengths. They usually look like ordinary elliptical galaxies in photographs. Radio telescopes detect two huge patches sending out radio signals on opposite sides of a central visible galaxy.

Astronomers suspect that violent events in the center of peculiar galaxies cause their exceptional energy output.

Galaxies such as M82 in Ursa Major and M87 in Virgo look as if a great explosion threw out high-speed gas streamers. Exploding galaxies are exceptionally bright in radio, infrared, or X-ray wavelengths.

Hundreds of pairs of galaxies look as if they are passing close to each other or even colliding. Their clouds of gas and dust are unusually dense. Many new stars and planets are probably being formed in those clouds.

Many things about galaxies remain a puzzle, but galaxies are not the only puzzling space objects. In ordinary photographs a quasar, or quasi-stellar object, looks like a star. In 1963 astronomer Maarten Schmidt proved that quasars could not be stars.

Quasars are not much bigger than our solar system. Yet they shine brighter than the brightest galaxies that contain billions of stars. The quasars send out radio, visible, infrared, and high-energy waves.

Quasars, like everything else in outer space, are continually on the move. They seem to be moving much faster than anything else in the universe.

Quasars also appear to be extremely far out in the universe. Apparently they are farther away from Earth than any other objects that have so far been detected. The farthest quasar observed seems to be 15 billion light-years away from Earth.

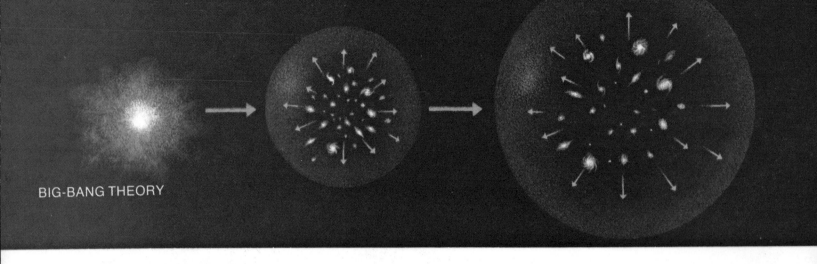

BIG-BANG THEORY

The Universe

EVERYTHING THAT SCIENTISTS know about the galaxies in our universe is determined from the radiation that they send out. Visible galaxies send out light from the billions of stars they contain, and their spectrums appear as dark lines on a bright background (see page 29).

The dark lines of distant galaxies are shifted toward the long wavelength, or red end, of the spectrum. This is called redshifted. The light from the faintest, most distant galaxies is redshifted the most. The redshift most likely means that other galaxies are racing away from ours.

Everywhere the giant telescopes can see in space, distant galaxies are apparently moving away from us. In 1929 Edwin Hubble found that the farther away a galaxy is from Earth, the faster it is traveling away from us. This relation is known as the Hubble law.

Our Galaxy is not the center of the universe. Stargazers in other galaxies would have the same view: they would see other galaxies speeding away from them. The universe is spreading out in all directions.

Most astronomers think that between 10 and 20 billion years ago, all matter in the universe was packed tightly together. It was unbelievably dense and hot. Our universe began when that fireball exploded. Bits of matter, blazing light, and heat waves shot out. This explanation of the universe is called the big-bang theory.

Ever since that first gigantic blast our universe has been spreading out. The initial supply of matter and energy has been recycled many times. Galaxies, stars, and planets have been formed from it.

Scientists consider the future of our universe. They expect it to go on as it is for at least another 40 billion years. The galaxies might continue to race apart forever. Then the original hydrogen would finally be used up in making new stars. The last stars would shine and go out. Our universe would become dark, cold, and lifeless.

Another possibility is that the force of gravity might slow the galaxies down enough to stop them. Then they would fall back together to form another superhot, superdense glob. It would explode in a new big bang. A new expanding universe would then be born and everything would start all over again.

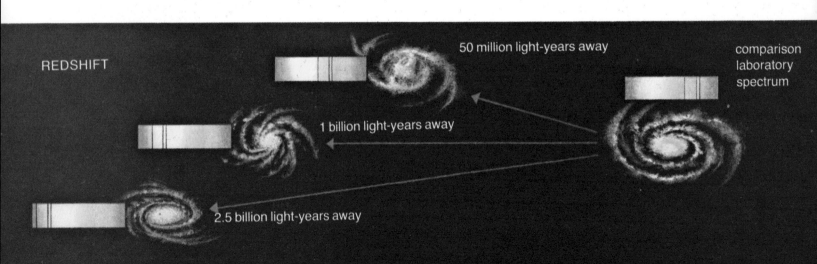

REDSHIFT

50 million light-years away

comparison laboratory spectrum

1 billion light-years away

2.5 billion light-years away

INDEX

References to pictures are in *italic type.*

Absolute magnitude, 86, *86–87*
Adams, John, 60
Ahnighito meteorite, 67, *67*
air, 38, 46
Algol, 87
Alpha Centauri, 84, *91*
Altair, *91*
Amalthea, 53
Amata, 56
amino acids, in meteorites, 66
Amor, *63*
annular eclipse, 41, *41*
A-1 Sputnik (USSR), *18*
A-1 Vostok (USSR), *18*
apogee, 20, *20*
Apollo missions, 39, *39, 44–45,* 45
Apollo objects (asteroids), 63, *63*
Apollo-Soyuz mission (USA–USSR), 69, *69*
Apollo spacecraft, 45, *45*
apparent magnitude, 85
Ariane 1 (ESA), *19*
Armstrong, Neil, 39, 69
asteroids, 22, *22–23,* 23, *62,* 63, *63*
astrology, 79
astronauts, 68–69
    Apollo, 39, *39, 44,* 45
    space shuttle, 73, 77, *77*
atmosphere, 25
    of Earth, 38, *38*
    of Neptune, 60
aurora australis (southern lights), 26
aurora borealis (northern lights), 26
auroras, 35, 38, *38*
axis:
    of Earth, 12, *12, 13*
    of Uranus, 59, *59*

Balloons, 15, 18, 19, *19*
Barnard's star, *91*
Barringer Crater, 67, *67*
Betelgeuse, 78, 86
big-bang theory, 94, *94*
Big Dipper, 84, *84,* 85, *85*
binary stars, *86,* 87, *87,* 89
binoculars, 16, *16*
Black Arrow (UK), *19*
black dwarf stars, 89
black holes, 89
blue supergiant stars, 86
Brand, Vance D., 69

Callisto, 52, 53, *53*
Caloris Basin, 30–31
canyons, on Mars, 49, *49*

Carr, Gerald P., 69
centripetal force, 23, *23*
Cepheid variables, 87
Ceres, 63, *63*
Charon, 61, *61*
chemical rockets, 18
Chiron, 63
Christy, James W., 61
chromosphere, *28,* 29
circular orbit, 20, *20*
clouds:
    of Earth, 25
    of Jupiter, 51, 52
    of Uranus, 59
    of Venus, 25, 32
clusters:
    of galaxies, 92
    of stars, 90, 91, *91*
coma (halo), 64, 65, *65*
comets, 22, 23, *64–65,* 65
communications satellites, 20–21
constellations, 78–79, *78–83*
continental drift, 36–37
convective zone, *28,* 29
core, Earth's, 35, *35*
corona, solar, 27, *27–29,* 29
craters:
    on Jupiter's moons, 52, 53
    on Mars, 49
    on Mercury, 30–31, *30–31*
    meteorite, 66, 67, *67*
    on Moon, 39, *39, 42–43*
    on Saturn's moons, 56, 57
crust, Earth's, 35, *35*
Cygnus, *78*
Cygnus X-1, 89

Day, 22
    night and, 8–9, *8, 9,* 12, 13, *13*
daylight-saving time, 9
Deimos, 47
Delphinus, *78*
delta Cephei, 87
density, of planets, 25. *See also individual planets*
Diamant BP4 (France), *19*
Dione, 56, *56,* 57
D-l-e Zond (USSR), *19*
Draco, *78*

Earth, 22, 24, *24,* 25, 35–38
    atmosphere of, 38, *38*
    axis of, 12, *12,* 13
    changing view of sky from, 10, 11, *11*
    continents of, 36–37
    core of, 35, *35*
    crust of, 35, *35*
    day and night on, 8–9, *8, 9*

formation of, 35
gravity of, 35
life on, 35
magnetic field of, 35
mantle of, 35, *35*
orbit of, 10, 11, *11–13,* 47, *47*
rotation of, 8
seasons of, 12, 13, *13*
as seen from Moon, 35, 37, *37*
solar wind around, *34,* 35
earthquakes, 36, *36,* 37
eclipse, 40–41, *41*
eclipsing binaries, 86, *86,* 87
Einstein, Albert, 88
elliptical galaxies, 92, *92*
elliptical orbits, 20, *20*
Enceladus, *56,* 57
Enke, comet, *65*
equinoxes, 12
Eros, 63
eruptive variables, 87
Europa, 52, 53, *53*
Europa 11 (ELDO), *19*
Evening Star, 33
Explorer 35 (USA), *43,* 43
extraterrestrial life, 46, 49, 90

Fireballs, 66
flares, solar, 26, 27, *26–27*
Freedom 7 (USA), *68,* 69
Friendship 7 (USA), *68,* 69
fuel, rocket, 18, *19*

Gagarin, Yuri, 69
galaxies, 7, 92–94, *92, 93.* *See also* Milky Way Galaxy
Galilean moons, 52. *See also* moons, of Jupiter
Galilei, Galileo, 39, 52, 55
Galle, Johann, 60
gamma rays, 14, 15, *15*
Ganymede, 23, 52, 53, *53*
Gemini 4 (USA), 69, *69*
Gibson, Edward G., 69
Glenn, John H., 69
Goodricke, John, 87
granules, 26
gravitation, Newton's law of, 87
gravity:
    Earth's, 35
Great Red Spot (Jupiter), 51
greenhouse effect, 32
ground stations, 15, *15*

Hall, Asaph, 47
Hall crater, 47
Halley, comet, *65*
halo (coma), 64, 65, *65*
helium, in Sun, 26
Hercules, 84
Herschel, Caroline, 87

Herschel, William, 87, 92
Hertzsprung, Ejnar, 86
Hidalgo, *63*
High Energy Astronomy Observatories, 15, *15*
highlands, of Moon, 39
Hipparchus, 85
Hoba West meteorite, 67
Holmes, comet, *65*
H-R (Hertzsprung-Russell) diagrams, 86, *86–87*
Hubble, Edwin, 92, 94
Hubble law, 94
Huygens, Christian, 55
Hyperion, 56, *57*
hydrogen, in Sun, 26

Iapetus, 56, *57*
Ikeya-Seki, comet, *65*
infrared rays, 14, *14*
International Ultraviolet Explorer, 15, *15*
Io, 52, *52,* 53, *53*
ionosphere, 38
irregular galaxies, 92, *92*
Ithaca Chasma, 56

Johnson Space Center (Texas), 73
Juno 1 (USA), *18*
Jupiter, 22–25, *23, 24,* 50, 51, *51*
    moons of, 51–53, *52–53*

Kant, Immanuel, 92
Kohoutek, comet, *65*
Komarov, Vladimir M., 69
Kubasov, Valery, 69
Kuiper Airborne Observatory, 59

Launch vehicles, 18, *18–19*
lava, in Mercury's craters, 31
LDEF (Long Duration Exposure Facility), 77, *77*
Leonov, Alexei A., 69
Lepus, *78*
Leverrier, Urbain, 60
light. *See* starlight; sunlight
light-year, 14
liquid fuel rockets, 18
Local Group, 92, 93, *93*
Lowell, Percival, 47, 61
luminosity of stars, 85–87
lunar eclipse, 41, *41*
lunar orbiter craft, *42–43,* 43
Luna (USSR) space probes to Moon, *42,* 43, *43*
Lunokhod 1 (USSR), *43,* 43
Lyra, 85

McMath Solar Telescope (Arizona), 26, 27, *26–27*

magnetic field:
    of Earth, 35
    of Jupiter, 51
    of Saturn, 55
magnetosphere, 34, *34,* 35
magnitudes of stars, 85, 86, *86–87*
main sequence, 86, *86*
manned maneuvering unit, 77, *77*
mantle, Earth's, 35, *35*
maria (seas), 39, *42–43*
Mariner (USA) space probes, 31, 48
Mariner Valley (Mars), *49*
Mars, 23, *23,* 24, *24,* 46–49, *47*
    "canals" (channels) on, 47, 49, *49*
    living organisms on, 46, 49
    moons of, 47
    orbit of, 47, *47*
    robot exploration of, 48–49, *48*
mass, 25
Maxwell Montes, 33
Mercury, *22,* 23, 24, *24,* 25, 30–31, *30–31*
Mercury-Atlas (USA), *19*
Mercury-Redstone (USA), *19*
meridians, 9
mesosphere, 38
meteorites, 66, 67, *67*
    Mercury's craters formed by, *30–31,* 31
meteoroids, 23, 66, *66*
meteors, 66–67
micrometeorites, on Moon, 39
Mid-Atlantic Ridge, 36
mid-ocean ridges, 36, *36*
Milky Way Galaxy, *6–7,* 7, 90, *90–91,* 91
Mimas, *56,* 57
Mira, 87
Mizar, 87
Moon, 39–43
    Apollo astronauts on, 39, *39*
    Apollo missions to, 39, *39, 44–45,* 45
    craters on, 39, *39, 42–43*
    eclipse of, 41, *41*
    map of, 39, *42–43*
    maria (seas) of, 39, *42–43*
    ocean tides and, 40, 41, *41*
    phases of, 39, 40, *40*
    probes to, 21, *21*
    robot explorations of, *42–43,* 43
    rocks of, 39
moons (of planets other than Earth), 23–25
    of Jupiter, 51–53, *52–53*

of Mars, 47
of Neptune, 60
of Saturn, 56–57, *56–57*
of Uranus, *58,* 59
Morning Star, 33
mountain ranges, 37, *37*
on Moon, 39, *42–43*
mountains:
formation of, 36, *36,* 37, *37*
on ocean bottom, 36, *36*
Mount Hopkins (Arizona)
telescope, 17, *17*
Mount Olympus (Mars), *49*
Mount Pastukhov (USSR),
Special Astrophysical
Observatory on, 17
Mount Wilson (California)
telescope, 92
Multiple Mirror Telescope
(MMT), 17, *17*
Mu-3H (Japan), *19*

Nebulas, 88, *88,* 89
of galaxies, 92
of Milky Way Galaxy, 90
Neptune, *22,* 24, 25, *25,* 60
Nereid, 60
neutron stars, 89, *89*
night and day, 8–9, *8, 9,*
12, 13, *13*
noon, 9
northern lights (aurora
borealis), 26
North Star (Polaris), 79, *79,* 84
novas, 87
nuclear fusion, 26, 84, 88, *89*
nucleus, of comet, 65, *65*

Ocean tides, 40, 41, *41*
Olympus Mons (Mars), 49
optical telescopes, 16, *16,*
17, *17*
orange giant stars, 86
orbit:
of asteroids, *63*
of Earth, 10, 11, *11–13*
of Mars, 47, *47*
of planets, 22–23, *23*
of satellites, 20–21, *20*
of Uranus, 59, *59*
Orion, 78, *78*

Palomar Mountain
(California) telescope,
17, *17*
Pangaea, 37, *37*
payload specialists, space
shuttle, 73
Pegasus, *78*
perigee, 20, *20*
phases of Moon, 39, 40, *40*
Phobos, 47
Phoebe, 56, *57*
photosphere, *28,* 29

Pioneer 10 (USA), 51, 61
Pioneer 11 (USA), 51
Pioneer Venus 1, 33
planetary nebulas, 89
planets, 22–25, *22–25*
probes to, 21, *21–23*
*See also individual
planets*
plates, 36, *36–37*
Pluto, 22, 23, *23,* 25, *25,*
61, *61*
Pogue, William R., 69
Polaris (North Star), 79,
79, 84
polar orbit, 20, *20*
Popov, Leonid, 69
probes, 21, *21–23*
Procyon, *91*
prominence, 29, *29*
propellants, 18
Proxima Centauri, 84
Ptolemy, 78
pulsars (pulsating radio
stars), 89, *89*

Quasars, 93

Radiative zone, *28,* 29
radio signals from galaxies,
93
radio telescopes, 14, *14*
radio waves, 14, *14,* 38
Ranger 7 (USA), *42,* 43
red dwarf stars, 85, 86, *87*
red giant stars, 89, *89*
redshifting, 94, *94*
red supergiant stars, 86
reflecting telescope, 16, *16,*
17, *17*
refracting telescope, 16, *16*
Rhea, 56, *57*
Riccioli, Giovanni, 87
rich clusters, 92
rings:
around Jupiter, 51
around Saturn, *54–55,* 55
around Uranus, *58,* 59
robot spacecraft (robot explorers), 33, *42–43,* 43
on Mars, 48–49, *48*
rockets, 18, *18–19,* 19
Russell, Henry Norris, 86
Ryumin, Valerii, 69

Salyut 1 (USSR), 71
Salyut 6 (USSR), 69, *69–71*
satellites, orbits of, 20–21,
20
Saturn, *22,* 23, 24, *24–25,*
55, 57
moons of, 56–57, *56–57*
rings around, *54–55,* 55
Saturn V Apollo (USA), *18*
Saturn V rocket, 45

Schiaparelli, Giovanni, 47
Schmidt, Maarten, 93
Scorpius, *78*
seasons, 12, *12, 13,* 46
seismographs, 36
Shepard, Alan, 69
''shooting stars,'' 66
Sirius, *91*
61 Cygni, *91*
Skylab, *68,* 69, 71
solar corona, 27, *27–29,* 29
solar eclipse, 40–41, *41*
solar energy, 26
solar flares, 26, 27, *28*
Solar Maximum Mission
spacecraft, 27, *27*
Solar Maximum Year
(1980–1981), 26
solar system, *6–7,* 7,
22–23, *22–23*
in orbit around center of
Galaxy, 90
solar wind, 26, *34,* 35
solid fuel rockets, 18
southern lights (aurora
australis), 26
Soyuz 1 (USSR), *68,* 69
space, changing view of,
10, 11, *11*
spacecraft. *See* robot
spacecraft
Spacelab, 73
space shuttle, *19,* 69, *69,*
72–77, *72, 74–77*
mission profile, 74–75,
74–75
space stations, 70, *70–71,*
71
space telescopes, 15, *15,*
17, *17*
space travel. *See* astronauts
spectrum, visible, 14, *15*
spiral galaxies, 92, *92*
Stafford, Thomas P., 69
stages of launch vehicles,
18, *19*
standard time, 9
stargazing, 78–83
starlight, 14, 15, *14–15*
star maps, 10, 79–83,
80–83
stars, 84–91
binary, *86,* 87, *87*
black dwarf, 89
blue supergiant, 86
changing view of space
and, 10, 11, *11*
clusters of, 90, 91, *91*
colors of, 84–85
composition of, 29
constellations of, 78–79,
78–83
death of, 88–89

distances from Earth, 84
evolution of, 88–89,
88–89
H-R (Hertzsprung-
Russell) diagrams of,
86, *86–87*
luminosity of, 85–87
magnitude (brightness)
of, 85, 86, *86–87*
main sequence of, 86, *86*
in Milky Way Galaxy,
90, 91, *91*
''moving'' across sky,
8–10
neutron, 89, *89*
novas, 87
nuclear fusion reactions
in, 84, 88, 89
orange giant, 86
positional changes of, 84,
85, *85*
pulsars, 89, *89*
red dwarf, 85, 86, *87*
red giant, 89, *89*
red supergiant, 86
sizes of, *84–85,* 85
space between, 90
temperature of, 84–85
variable, 87
white dwarf, 86, 89
stratosphere, 38, *38*
Sun, 24, *24–25,* 26–29,
28–29, 84
brightness of, 85
Earth's orbit around, 10,
11, *11–13*
eclipse of, 40–41, *41*
energy of, 26, 29
formation of, 88
hydrogen and helium in, 26
''moving'' across sky, 8
orbits of planets around,
22–23, *23*
spin of, 29
temperature of, 26, 29
sunlight, 8, *8,* 9, *9,* 26
colors of, 14
seasons and, 12, 13, *13*
sunrise and sunset, 8, *8,* 9, *9*
sunspots, 26, 29, *29*
superclusters, 92–93
supernovas, 89, *89*
Surveyor spacecraft (USA),
42, 43
synchronous orbits, 20–21,
20

Telescopes
radio, 14, *14*
solar, 26, 27, *26–27*
on space stations, 71
starlight collected with,
14, *14*

Tempel-2, comet, *65*
Tereshkova, Valentina, 69
Tethys, 56
thermosphere, *38*
tides, ocean, 40, 41, *41*
tilt, of Earth, 12, 13, *13*
time, 9
time zones, 9
Titan, 56, 57, *57*
Titan 111 E-Centaur
(USA), *19*
Tombaugh, Clyde, 61
Triton, 60
troposphere, 38, *38*

Universe, 94
Uranus, *22,* 23, 24, *25,* 59,
59
Ursa Major, *78*

Valles Marineris (Mars), *49*
Van Allen belts, *34,* 35
Van Maanen's star, *91*
variable stars, 87
Vega, 85
Venera (USSR) space
probes, 33
Venus, 22–25, *23, 24,*
32–33, *32–33*
Very Large Array (New
Mexico), 14
Vesta, *63*
Viking 1 (USA), *46,* 48, 49
Viking 2 (USA), 48
Viking space probes, 49
Virgo supercluster, 92, 93
visible light, 14, *15,* 29
visual binary, 87
volcanoes:
on Earth, 36, *36,* 37
on Mars, 49, *49*
Voskhod 2 (USSR), *68,* 69
Vostok 1 (USSR), *68,* 69
Vostok 6 (USSR), *68,* 69
Voyager 1 (USA), 51, 53
path of, 60, *60*
Saturn's rings as seen
from, *54–55,* 55
Voyager 2 (USA), *50,* 51,
59, 60, *60*

Water:
on Earth, 35
on Mars, 46–47, 49
Wegener, Alfred, 36
weightlessness, 71
Whipple, Fred, 64
White, Edward H., 11, 69
white dwarf stars, 86, 89

X rays, 14, 15, *15*

Years, 23

Zodiac, constellations of,
79, *79*